TOIL & TRUFFLE

A Gloam HOLLOW

COZY WITCH MYSTERY

BOOK ONE

JANE LENORE

For more information, address: jlvampa@jlvampa.com.

First edition September 2024

Cover by J.L. Vampa — www.jlvampa.com
Character Art by Yulia Volska
Gloam Hollow Square by Anastasiia K

TikTok: @jlvampa

Paperback ISBN 979-8-3303-1130-9
Ebook AISN B0D94V2S5Y

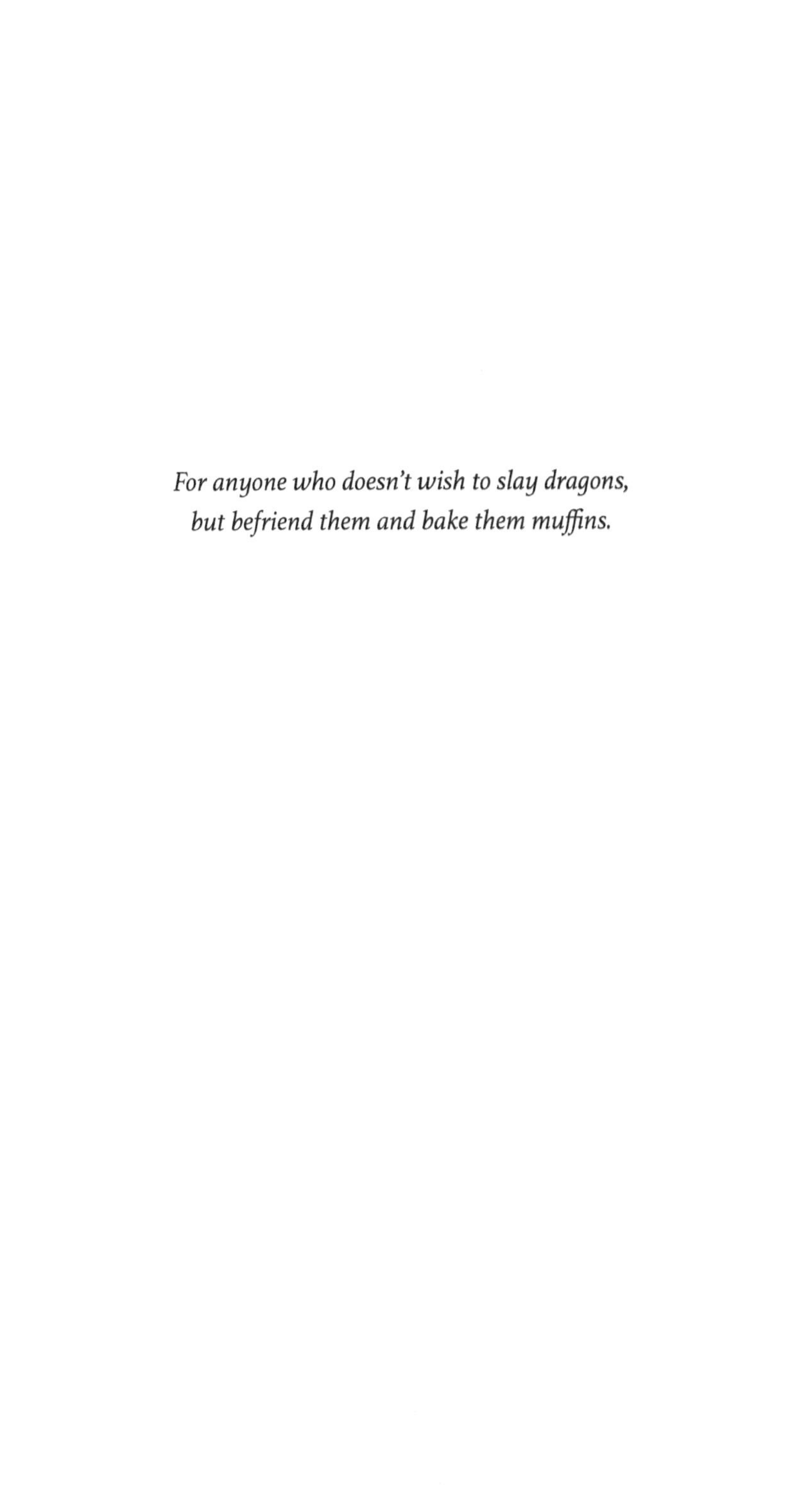

For anyone who doesn't wish to slay dragons,
but befriend them and bake them muffins.

Spectre
Café

THE
SPECTRE
CAFÉ
SUGAR HOLLOW
CANDY SHOPPE
Broom & Blossom Florist
Gloam Hollow

ENJOY

Gloam HOLLOW

RECIPES

in the back of the book

TOIL & TRUFFLE

A Gloam HOLLOW

COZY WITCH MYSTERY

BOOK ONE

CHAPTER 1

As soon as my feet hit the floor, I knew.

I knew he'd done it again.

Launching out of bed, I threw on my black silk robe and flung open the door. Tearing down the stairs, I sent magic out to amplify my voice to every cobwebbed corner of the cottage.

At the last step, I grabbed the carved knob of the post, flinging myself around and into a run. "*Hamish!*" I bellowed, slamming into the sideboard as I scuttled my way through the entry. I had not taken the time to put on my glasses that I very much needed to see, and glass baubles crashed to the floor in my wake.

"Hamish don't you *dare!*" I skidded to a stop in the kitchen and his eyes went wide, then sinister before he took off at a run through the archway leading into the dining room.

With a growl of frustration, I followed, bare feet slapping over the hardwood. "Coward!" I shouted after him. "If you so much as thi—" I screeched as my feet left the ground in a rush and I was levitating over my grandmother's dining table, the old brass chandelier knocking into the back of my head.

Hamish laughed viciously.

I canceled out his spell with one of mine, simultaneously causing a lump in the rug that made him trip as he attempted to flee my wrath. He fell flat on his back and slid into the living area with an *oomph*, nearly dropping my quarry as he smacked into the floral-patterned sofa.

I floated down to the ground and stood over him, a wisp of glimmering magic slithering from my fingertip. "Give it here."

"You're insane, Blair." Hamish scrabbled to his feet, his sweater vest and cravat askew.

Behind him, a girlish giggle erupted from the back porch. "Never get between a Witch and the last donut, Hamish," Maggie tutted as the screen door squeaked on its hinges and she stepped into the cottage. "Thought you would have learned that by now."

"Pick a side, Mags," I urged, the door smacking shut behind her.

"Puh-lease." She flung herself onto the sofa and set to sipping her coffee, one pinky high in the air. "I'm not getting in the middle of this. You two may have forgotten, but I remember well the Great Donut Disaster of three years ago."

That dark day was seven shades of fuzzy in my memory. All I recall is waking up on Draak Summit in the middle of the night, freezing cold, and hurriedly getting off the mountain before the Dragon came back to slumber at dawn.

My lip pulled back in a sneer at the only other memory from that day: Hamish waking up dazed in the middle of the

Gloam Hollow Cemetery, clothed only in his underwear and chicken feathers.

A *lot* of chicken feathers.

"Let's not repeat the feathers incident," I goaded him.

"Why?" he spat right back. "Afraid of heights?" He risked a tiny step closer. "Or Dragons?"

I muttered in frustration, my wisp of magic still poised. "I will singe holes in that sweater vest, Hamish. Don't test me. *Give me* the donut."

"You could try asking nicely," he ground out, hiding the stolen confection behind his back.

"Ha!" Maggie shouted from her position of *not getting involved*. "Because that worked so well the last time."

Hamish twisted toward our roommate—who happened to also be our cousin—revealing the donut and its chocolate glaze perilously close to sliding off. His face contorted in righteous indignation. "Blair wouldn't know what it was to ask nicely if it bit her in the—"

I pounced.

Magic shot out of my hands as I leaped onto Hamish's back, one coil wrapping around the donut to whisk it high in the air to safety, another coil wrapping around Hamish's ankles.

"Blair!" he bellowed as he toppled over onto the couch—also belonging to our grandmother, the whole place did, in fact.

I cackled, reeling in my prize, but magic burst from Hamish, encasing the donut in a protective shield, like a glistening soap bubble. Growling and done with playing nice, I conjured a cluster of spiders right on top of Hamish's chest.

He screamed—the high-pitched sort reserved for

teenage girls—and whacked at his chest just long enough for his concentration to drop on his protective bubble spell. I lunged for the donut, catching it just before it landed in Maggie's wild curls.

"Truce!" Hamish shouted, still swatting at the spindly arachnids while I licked chocolate off my thumb. "Truce! I'll clean the upstairs cat boxes for a week if you'll just *get these off me!*"

Did I mention Hamish is deathly afraid of spiders? Peculiar phobia for a Warlock, if you ask me. But here we are.

You probably think I'm sadistic, a bully. I assure you it's not true. But when your Witch mothers are as close of sisters as ours are, you become siblings at the best of times and...siblings at the worst of times. Especially when your grandmother and mother decide to take up residence in the family inn, and suddenly you're in charge of an entire old cottage. Naturally, you wrangle your "siblings" into being your roommates.

But...things can get a bit out of hand.

Case in point: Last week, Hamish laced my toothpaste with Star Salamander slime and I hallucinated for three days. Two of those days I was convinced I was the master of a carnival circus.

Hamish deserved a little payback.

Besides, it's not like I was going to let the *magical* spiders bite him. Just...give him nightmares for a few moon cycles.

"Blair," Maggie warned, and I rolled my eyes. She was always the voice of reason between the three of us. She snatched the donut from me and balanced it on her empty coffee mug, then gave me a wide-eyed head tilt that clearly meant: *end this.*

I crossed my arms and shrugged at Hamish as he flailed on the sofa. "You have to clean the downstairs boxes, too. You only chose upstairs because of Chester. Ghost cats don't poop."

Chester did, however, have a litter box he apparently brought with him into the astral realm, and we went through the motions—at his behest—of cleaning it.

Hamish shivered and made a horrified, garbley noise as he flicked a spider off his cheek. "Fine! All the boxes."

"For an entire moon cycle."

"Blair, come on," Maggie cut in.

"I'll do it! Just get these off me!"

I snapped my fingers and the little harmless spiders were gone in puffs of fog.

A whoosh of air left Hamish as he sat up, brushing off his vest. I bent down and retrieved his precious cravat that had fallen off in the hubbub. (Hamish is always dressed to the nines like his mother, my Aunt Moira.) He glared at me as he took it.

"Maybe you won't take my donut next time." We traded wholly immature faces, tongues out and eyes crossed before I padded my way over to the back stairs.

"Oh, hey," Maggie said as I reached the third step up. "We had something come up and Stacey needs me to work late at the salon. Can one of you make dinner?"

"Your name is on the calendar." Hamish chopped one hand with the other. "That means you make the dinner."

"Obviously I can't if I have to work."

In the way of sibling-esque relationships, Hamish had already forgotten our squabble and was looking over the back of the sofa at me with *back-me-up* energy.

Unfortunately—our squabble not considered—I was

still on Maggie's side. "Sometimes things come up and we have to be flexible. If you had to work late at the library, I would cover your chores. It's what roommates do."

"Does that mean you'll cook tonight?" Hamish asked, his voice dripping with disdain.

I winced and made a clicking sound with my tongue and cheek. "Can't. It's book club night."

Hamish dropped his head into his hands, his voice muffled as he said, "First I don't get the donut, then I have to clean all the litter boxes for an entire moon cycle, and now I have to make dinner, too?"

I'd like to take this moment to explain that we are not teenagers. Nor are we *young* adults. You might have gotten that impression by how juvenile we act, but, I assure you, we are proper adults, all three of us. Have been for some time.

And we really do care about each other.

"I'll tell ya' what," I said, descending the stairs and coming to ruffle his dark hair. "You make something simple for dinner tonight and when it's finally open in a couple weeks, we'll go out to that new mysterious café. My treat."

Hamish lifted his head and turned to look at me with suspicion. "This better not be a ploy to stick me with the check at the end of dinner."

I balked, affronted. "Excuse me, I would never!"

"You did once," he shot back.

"Because I forgot my wallet!"

"Mmhmm."

He and Maggie shared a look and I knew exactly what their silent conversation was about.

"The apothecary is doing *just fine*, thank you very much."

Maggie snorted and I whirled on her. She tucked her lips between her teeth.

Angry with them both all over again, I snatched my hard-won donut I'd forgotten to grab, and stomped off toward my room. I bit into the donut, the salted caramel and chocolate colliding with soft pastry. It was worth every bit of drama getting it back.

I was still mad about the apothecary insinuations, though.

Brewing potions for a living in a town filled with magical beings was often...unnecessary, and my income was forever fluctuating. A few years ago, I'd added some books for sale and that helped business for a while. That was until the town's most popular coffee shop on the square began offering a book-lending service.

Licking the remaining chocolate glaze from my fingertips, I put on my glasses. I flopped down on the corner of the bed and blew the hair out of my eyes, blinking a few times to refocus my vision.

Lacuna, the owner of *Stonewood Brews*, is a dear friend of mine and I'd encouraged her idea to start lending out books. It was a good plan, and I didn't want to stand in the way of it. However, between her book lending and the Gloam Hollow Library, I'd lost almost all of that part of my business, too.

Closing down *The Copper Cauldron Apothecary and Bookshop* wasn't an option for me. It felt like giving up, like a failure. But it was time to face the music if things didn't turn around soon.

I pushed my depressing thoughts and heinous morning aside and rose. A day is what you make it, and I was determined to focus on the good.

Nodding resolutely at my reflection, I set to brushing the stubborn tangles out of my fiery hair. I considered fighting with eyeliner, but it was always so *fussy*. Thus, I settled for a smidge of glimmering eyeshadow and mascara, with a dark lipstick called *Vampiric Plum* that perfectly matched my fingernails.

Pleased as punch, I put my circular, wire-framed glasses back on and went to stand before my racks of clothing—I like my favorite outfits right where I can see them. After careful consideration, I elected to wear a black a-line skirt patterned with moody florals. It was just long enough to brush my ankles and it boasted a slit all the way to the middle of my thigh.

A finger tapping my lip, I pondered over which top to pair with it. Option one would result in a lecture from my mother or aunts, despite having been on my own for a very long time. Option two made me feel a little self-conscious, but it was *so* perfect.

In the end, I went for option two. A snug, black crop top that hugged me in all the right places and left a sliver of skin showing at my midriff. I'm a curvy witch, and the outfit made me look amazing, but that dash of self-consciousness snuck right in.

I grabbed an oversized olive cardigan to throw over the top. There. Still stylish, still a pinch daring, but I could hide behind the sweater if I needed to retreat into myself.

I frowned. It covered my smattering of dainty floral tattoos, though. The weather in The Hollow was still warm, too, not yet cool enough for a sweater. And wasn't I trying to be more self-assured?

"Bah!" I took off the cardigan and tossed it on the bed.

My messenger bag had evidently been thrown on the ground with great care last night, considering it was in a heap on my rug, its contents spilling out. I placed everything back inside that needed to stay, only trading out two books for two others—I'm a mood reader, what can I say? Then, I added in the book club pick and one other book I'd just finished per Lacuna's recommendation. I'd drop it off at *Stonewood* on my way to work.

Once my strappy black platforms were on, I slipped my bag across my body and was ready for the day.

I made it halfway down the stairs before I turned around and trotted back up. "Just in case," I whispered to myself as I retrieved my sweater and slung it across my bag.

CHAPTER 2

The door creaked as I opened it and stepped out onto the front steps. My grandmother's old cottage-turned-my-cottage might be past its prime, but it's much less ramshackle and much more picturesque. Tucked in a thicket of lush trees and covered in moss and ivy, the stone cottage is what Witch dreams are made of.

I took a deep breath, relishing the hint of cooler weather teasing at the breeze. We'd endured an unseasonably hot spell for quite some time, but the winds had changed and there was the barest dusting of fog clinging to the treetops this early in the morning.

In Gloam Hollow, we never exactly knew when the weather would turn, for how long, or in which direction it would go. Sometimes, summer would follow winter, or spring might turn to autumn and back again in the span of a moon cycle. I don't know a great deal about the Mortal Lands, but between my studies and the fact-spouter that is Hamish, I've gathered that their seasons go in some sort of order and are more or less predictable. Not here.

Gloam Hollow might be home to a plethora of magical beings and is usually a sleepy, mountainside town, but its unpredictability happens to be one of my favorite things about it. You never quite know what might happen.

Halfway down the cobble and dirt path toward our tree tunnel street, I felt a little brush of fur against my toes, followed by loud purring near my feet.

"Hello, you," I cooed, bending down to scratch Albis between his ears, his shaggy gray fur soft as cattail fluff. Soon enough, Puck and Beetle joined in the fray, wanting their turn and squabbling with one another, not unlike Hamish and I earlier. I chuckled to myself. It was fitting, really. Albis had the silvery fur of Maggie's wild curls, Beetle had the same fur coloring as Hamish's jet-black hair, and ornery Puck was a ginger, like yours truly.

You got pets first last time! Beetle was saying.

Who cares! Puck meowed right back.

I was here first! Albis hissed, swatting at them.

No, the cats don't speak like we do, but, as a Witch, I can understand them. As far as I know, all Witches and Warlocks can understand either cats, bats, or owls. The very lucky few can understand all three. I happen to be one of those lucky few, and quite thankful for it.

"Now, now," I censured the cats lightly. "We don't swat and hiss at our friends. Think how sweet Chester feels, not getting any pets at all because he's a *ghost*."

It wasn't my brightest method of breaking up a catfight, nor would I call it tactful, but it worked. They all three hung their heads and trotted back toward the cottage, presumably to beg Maggie for food or keep Chester company. The poor guy couldn't leave the top floor. He was my great-great grandmother's tabby cat from who knows how long ago, and when he died he just...stuck around. He's been at Wardwell Cottage ever since.

I stood and dusted kitty paw prints off my skirt and bid the cottage farewell until evening. It would be a long day, but I was looking forward to every bit of it.

With it being fairly early in the morning still, the sidewalk was empty of anyone else until I made it almost to the square. Since Gloam Hollow is relatively small, most of us walk—or occasionally fly—just about everywhere. Once the sun is well and truly shining above the tree line, things are lively until after it slips behind the mountains at night.

"Hi, Mrs. Winslow!" I waved at the antique shop owner as I passed.

At first, the Troll woman only scowled, looking up from in front of the shop with her hands on her hips. When she saw it was me, her face brightened.

"Blair!" She waddled over to the fence at the edge of her property. "I was just about to phone your Aunt Mildred. My Dragon Tulips died!" There was a hint of hysteria in her voice that was not unexpected from Mrs. Winslow, but I flinched anyway. "Just shriveled right up!"

I wasn't exactly sure what she'd expected considering the heatwave we'd had, but if it mattered to her then it mattered, period. "I'm so sorry, that's terrible," I told her in earnest.

"Would you be a dear and brew me a potion for it? Millie has been so busy at the florist, I don't think she'll have time to come save the wee things."

The prospect of a customer gave me a distinct urge to perk my ears like a cat who's heard the tuna can open. I dutifully resisted, playing the cool cucumber instead. "Oh, sure, I think I could find some time today at the apothecary to—"

"Great!" Mrs. Winslow cheered and gave a little hop. "Here." She dug around in her wide, unflattering... nightgown? dress? and produced far too many moonstones for a simple floral potion, handing them to me.

"Oh, I— Mrs. Winslow, this is too much." I was borderline desperate for money, but I was no con artist.

"Nonsense." She began wobbling away, waving at me over her shoulder. "Thank you, dear!"

Gaping down at the moonstones glistening in the light of the rising sun, a jubilance started at my toes and tingled all the way up to my ears, resulting in a smile. It was shaping up to be a fantastic day after all. I deposited the moonstones into the velvet pouch in my bag and ambled on.

Just past the corner of Maple Lane and Peach Street, the Gloam Hollow Square opened up in all its glory. I paused next to one of the many ornate lampposts and took in the sight of the sunrise still painting the sky in cotton candy clouds. Its rays lit the gazebo and surrounding green in hues not even magic could mimic.

On a deep inhale, I took a moment to appreciate my little haven. The striped awning of the grocer tucked up next to the coffee shop. The minuscule movie theater snuggled between the hardware store and an ice cream parlor. Across the square was my mom's *Toil & Truffle Bakery,* kitty-corner to my beloved apothecary, which sat right next to the mysterious new café set to open in a couple of weeks.

Sure, there was a wide, paranormal world out there and the Mortal Lands somewhere, too. But Gloam Hollow is my *home.* I wouldn't leave, even under penalty of death.

My smile twitched into deep sniffing. *"Coffee,"* I

breathed, letting my nose lead me to where the *Stonewood Brews* sign was swaying in the breeze. I paused on the step, one hand on the door handle. That tepid breeze was suddenly feeling quite brisk. A look over my shoulder revealed what I suspected: the leaves of trees lining the sidewalk were changing color and beginning to sway.

Autumn was slipping her magic into The Hollow.

This day just got better and better.

The bell above the door to *Stonewood* tinkled, and I breathed in deeply the aromas of coffee and cinnamon rolls, welcoming their embrace. Soon, the coffee shop would be bustling with activity until the mid-morning lull when I would *probably* be back to feed my coffee addiction.

I'd been planning to use the last of my funds from frog-sitting Mr. Pedigrew's pet, Marcus, last week to caffeinate myself, but with the moonstones from Mrs. Winslow, I was practically loaded.

"Morning, Blair!" a perky voice called from behind the counter. "Care for the usual?"

I smiled at Lacuna's flour-sprinkled face. Her velvety skin, the color of darkest night, always gave away signs of her most recent baking endeavor. Today, the Shadow Nymph had undoubtedly crafted the cinnamon roll delicacies herself rather than stocking her cases with baked goods from *Toil and Truffle*. If I'm not mistaken, Lacuna had been frosting cupcakes as well, if the bright color showing up as she wiped her hands on a rag was any indication.

"That'll be..."

"Thirty-six moonstones," I finished for her.

Lacuna smiled and held out a tattooed hand. The markings were difficult to see without focused inspection, but I knew many of them. Lacuna and I had been friends for ages since we were little bookish girls at Gloam Hollow Primary.

"Oh!" I fumbled around in my bag after I handed her the moonstones. "Sorry. Here is that book you lent me."

"What did you think?" Lacuna's amethyst-colored eyes had gone a bit wide, expectant, and I wrinkled my nose, my glasses shifting with the movement. I didn't want to disappoint her. I reserved all of that for Hamish and Maggie. "Hang on..." She bustled off to put my order ticket up on the string above the espresso machine and grabbed a hot pan of cinnamon rolls. "So?" she asked with a bright smile when she returned.

"I–" My shoulders fell. "Didn't love it. Solid three stars. I'm so sorry."

Lacuna only laughed, her glowing lilac hair swaying as she set out the rolls in her baked goods showcase. My friend is a vision. If you've never met a Shadow Nymph, they're all mesmerizing, but *Lacuna*? Unmatched.

"Katarina! Order up!" a perturbed voice called out, making Lacuna jump.

"Anon!" she chastised. "Why do you have to lurk? I could've burned myself on this pan."

Katarina bopped up to the counter, her platinum blonde bob bouncing and purple Pixie dust falling from her wings with every movement.

"Hi, Blair!" she quipped, ever-bubbly. "I was going to come by the apothecary today." She leaned in conspiratorially and Lacuna pretended not to listen in. "Did you hear George Carter's yard flamingo was stolen and Sheriff Oliphant found it on his roof?"

I snorted. "Yeah, I heard about that." Our kindly sheriff, Corbin Oliphant, had been less than amused by the prank.

"Would you be interested in making a statement for *The Gloam Reporter*? A stab at who the culprit was?" She waggled her eyebrows at me and I laughed.

"Sure, Kat. Come by later."

Katarina preened and strode to her usual cobalt couch in the corner, pulling out a shiny laptop and a notebook from her pink bag. She set to work on her latest news blog while Lacuna steamed milk for my coffee and put a fresh, gooey sweet roll on a plate for me, steam coiling into the air.

"Free of charge." Lacuna winked at me.

"Thanks, Lac."

"I hate when she comes in here," Anon griped from behind Lacuna. I looked over at the only other person in the place—Katarina.

"Kat?" I clarified anyway. Who didn't love Kat? Sure she was extra peppy and a little too into gossip, but she was a sweet girl.

"She comes in every day," Lacuna pointed out.

"Precisely." Anon adjusted his thick glasses on the bridge of his nose and grabbed a broom and dustpan. He gestured dramatically from the door to where Katarina sat leaning over the coffee table and her laptop. "There's a *trail* of Pixie dust from the front all the way to her, and a *pile* of it underneath her. Not to mention I have to vacuum that couch every day when she leaves."

Lacuna and I bit back our giggles as Anon stalked over and noisily swept up the Pixie dust, muttering as he did so. When he got to Katarina, he cleared his throat loudly and swept right underneath her without a word of explanation. Katarina, engrossed in her work, lifted her dainty feet without even glancing away from her furious typing.

He stomped back behind the counter, scowling. "You'd

think she'd at least pick up after herself or apologize. Those Faeries leave that sparkling mess everywhere they go. It's exhausting."

"There, there, Anon." Lacuna patted her co-worker and best friend on the shoulder. "Let's not discriminate against Faeries."

"Oh, here we go." Anon rolled his eyes. "You've spent far too much time studying the Mortal Lands. I'm not discriminating, Lacuna. I would just think some better measures would be in place for Faerie dust clean-up after, you know, *millennia*."

"Blair!" the other barista called out. "Order up!" He's a sweet-faced young teen you would never guess shifts into a Werewolf.

Lacuna was deep in debate with Anon over the lack of Faerie dust removal technology, so I slipped away, sliding my cinnamon roll plate down the counter. "Excuse me, Luke?"

The barista turned around, his cheeks going bright red when he saw me. "Morning, Blair. I like your outfit." His blush deepened and there was a great chance one was climbing up my neck at the awkward attention.

"Ah, thanks." I don't do well with awkward and considered bolting. Who needed coffee and a cinnamon roll, anyway? Oh, right. Me. "Could I get a carry-out box for my bun?" I held the plate aloft, and Luke took it, returning a moment later with one of those little bakery boxes that just makes everything feel sweeter. "Thanks, Luke."

As I passed by, I waved goodbye to Katarina who hardly looked up from the many devices laid out before her on the coffee table. "See ya', Blair!"

Lacuna gave me a half-wave, still deep in a whispered

fight with Anon, who looked as if he might shift at any moment.

Most of us in Gloam Hollow have more than one form, electing to remain in the most palatable one, which would be the one where we are most uniform. I guess you could say we look quite a lot like the humans in the Mortal Lands, or so I'm told. Some of us walk around trading our different skins like outfits, some have only subtle differences—like Lacuna's glowing hair and eyes, or the Vamps' elongated teeth—but then there are the ones like Anon and Luke. Anon is a Wendigo, and, to be frank, none of us like when he walks around like that, least of all Anon. It can be unnerving. Not because of what he looks like—which is somewhere between a moose skeleton and a half-turned Werewolf body—but because he's so at odds with that portion of himself. It's like watching a train wreck. He has to shift, though, or he'd forget how, so he usually goes out into the woods or up the mountains to stomp around. On some occasions, his state of constant agitation gets to him and the shift happens without warning. And it is destructive at best.

"Hey," I interrupted them, thinking better of leaving the coffee shop and its inhabitants to a potential Wendigo burst. "Maybe get some air, Anon. You're looking...peaked."

He appeared angry at first when Lacuna pursed her lips in a show of: *See what you've done?* But he caught sight of his hands, staring with wide eyes as his fingers elongated and his nails pointed. Risking a feel at his chin, he found more of what I was talking about—it had sharpened.

Lacuna's agitation dropped and she put a hand on Anon's shoulder. "Yeah, you're getting a bit shifty in the face, friend."

I could confirm, the telltale wobble and haze of an

impending shift was warbling his features. "Maybe take a walk."

"Yeah. Yeah, okay." Anon nodded too many times, untying his apron with difficulty. He laid it on the counter and headed for the door.

I said my goodbyes to Lacuna and followed him out, slipping ungracefully through the door before it could shut on me and spill my coffee. I made some muddled *eek* noise as the handle clipped my back and Anon turned around.

"I'm sorry, Anon. I didn't mean to be pushy," I said when I caught up to him.

"Do you think you could brew me some more potion for my anxiety?" he asked me sheepishly, still a little fuzzy in the face.

I'd plum forgotten I made that for him, he hadn't been into the apothecary in so long. "Absolutely. I'd be happy to. Is everything alright?" As far I could tell, Anon lived in a state of anxiousness, but he did seem a bit more on edge than usual.

He fumbled with his glasses, his face going a tick too wide and angular to keep them on. "Yeah, yes," he stammered, turning away and hurrying to cross the square where he would no doubt take a path leading up into the mountains.

"That was weird," I said to myself but shrugged it off.

I would no longer be piddling around my shop pretending I had things to do today. I had not one, but two special orders to make.

CHAPTER 3

I'd spent so much time in *Stonewood* this morning, that The Hollow had fully awoken by the time I left with coffee in hand. That meant I was stopped no less than six times in the span of the eight shops I had to pass to make it to *The Copper Cauldron.*

First, Kurt Rossenblossom—Goblin, looks like a Goblin—almost tripped me with his dog's leash outside the bank. Next, I was tangled up in a dispute over newspapers between Ms. Cooper—a terrifying Banshee who usually wore the face of an elderly woman—and Pepper Cornish—plain ol' Witch like me—outside the grocers. I did not help matters by suggesting Katarina's online news blog as an alternative to their dispute, even though I've never read it myself.

"*Pish!*" Ms. Cooper spat at me, spittle flying and everything. "You *young people* and your Interweb."

I did mention I'm not a *youth*, didn't I? In fact, I'm over a hundred in our years, but most of the town stopped counting age well before I was born. We tend to age in a peculiar fashion, yet somehow all together by generation. Ms. Cooper therefore thinks anyone younger than her is a '*street youth*' up to no good. Her phrasing, not mine. Although, I'm not certain she knows what a street youth is.

After Ms. Cooper and her age discrimination, there were three hellos to be had, one minor stop as I crossed the green to give our town busker under the gazebo a couple of my coveted moonstones—he's such a nice fellow, a Merman in his other form if you can believe it.

That left the stop at my mother's bakery.

"Blair!"

I winced and tried to hide my *Stonewood Brews* pastry box. "Hi, Mama."

She stomped out of *Toil & Trouble*, hands on her hips and apron as askew as her red hair. She'd likely already put in a full day's work baking before the rest of us rose from bed. "Is that a cinnamon roll?" Her eyes were squinted and glinty.

There is one thing you should know about my mother. She is sweet as pie, feisty when need be, and *everyone's* chosen mother. Unless you partake of a pastry *she* did not bake.

"Erm. Yes?"

"Lacuna Pindle!" she spat my friend's name like a curse.

And that was the end of our conversation. She was power-walking down the sidewalk toward *Stonewood*, ignoring everyone who tried to speak with her. I chuckled to myself and fiddled for my keys as I stepped off the curb and crossed the little corner of the street to my shop.

"Blair Wardwell!" another voice barked my name. "That is jaywalking what you just did."

Make that seven stops before making it to my shop. I

tilted my head back and groaned before turning to face my accuser. Bill Winslow. Town busybody. If I thought eyeliner was fussy, Bill was about a hundred times that.

His shiny shoes made a quick tattoo on the sidewalk as he approached me. "As Gloam Hollow Mayor, it is my duty to ensure all our citizens follow the letter of the law."

Oh yeah, he's the mayor, too. But he looks like a walrus. Which isn't that far off from how he looks in his Troll form. Mrs. Winslow is his mother, but aside from name and general Troll roundness, the character resemblance ends there.

"How did you become Mayor again, Bill? I can't recall." Of course I recalled. Six years ago, his opposition won by a largely unanimous vote, and then promptly lost his mind dealing with all the small-town madness that is Gloam Hollow. Bill took over by forfeit.

His face turned red and his huge mustache twitched. "Miss Wardwell, if I catch you not following the laws of this fine town, I *will* write you a citation."

Did he call me *Miss Wardwell* to try to convince me to call him *mister*? Not happening. "Bill, you're not the police. You can't write citations."

Somehow, his face reddened further, and I thought he might burst into flames or into Troll form. "Follow the laws," he ground out. "Good day."

Bill turned on his shiny heel and bustled off like a walking sea cow, his khaki dress pants swishing.

I still hadn't fished my keys out of my bag, so I just used a spell to open the lock to my apothecary. The hinges creaked as the door swung open—as any good Witchy shop door should—and I breathed in the scents of sage, patchouli, and ginger. The remnants of the last potion I'd brewed yesterday.

I sent little flames out from my palm to land in all the gas lamps, and upon all the many candle wicks. Once everything was aglow in a perfect blend of mood and warmth, I flipped my little window sign to *Open*. I might not see much business these days, but the place made me *happy*.

Though not a large building, *The Copper Cauldron* boasts six floor-to-ceiling shelves my grandfather built when it was his tea and smoke shop many decades ago. I didn't know if it was good or bad, telling of my shop's status or not, but every bit of space on those shelves was filled with potions. Too many to even count without losing my place.

Down the rows of shelves sits a small, wooden counter where I take orders and payments. But my favorite area of the shop lies in the opposite corner. A little nook of bookshelves overflowing with tomes old and new, in every genre imaginable. In front of them, I'd placed an ornate rug, upon which are two of the most comfortable wingback chairs one could fathom in deep, forest green velvet. A perfect cozy reading area in front of a classically Witchy hearth. There, the fires are completely magical, as I have no chimney. A small table stands between the chairs, waiting for someone to come sit, set down their coffee, and enjoy a book.

No one but me has sat there for ages.

I shook off the bit of melancholy that tried to sneak in and deposited my bag and sweater behind the counter. Glancing out the shop's giant front window overlooking the square, I noticed the trees had changed even more since I'd been at *Stonewood*.

A spark of hope settled in my chest. Perhaps my shop

had lain empty because the warm spell had most people outdoors. Hiking the mountain trails, playing frisbee on the green, picnics in Dew Park... Now that the seasons had decided to shift, maybe it would encourage the creatures of Gloam Hollow to don sweaters and curl up in bookish corners.

The apothecary door opened, a bang sounding when it slammed into the nearest shelf for opening too hard. I shot magic out toward the bottles of potions that nearly crashed to the floor. The sight reminded me I'd never cleaned up all the baubles I'd broken in the foyer this morning. *Whoops.*

"Oh," a deep voice said from the doorway. The juxtaposition of dimness within the apothecary and the brightness without gave me only a vague outline of a shadowy figure. Until he shut the door.

I schooled my features the best I could because *Goddess,* the stranger was handsome. Dark skin and bright green eyes, he was tall and bulky, but not in that overly muscled way of romance novels. His hair, or what I could see of it, was green like his eyes. I could tell it was styled in dreadlocks, but they were all tied on top of his head, a cloth covering them. He gave me a close-lipped smile and I had to swallow. That scruffy beard...

"Didn't mean to open the door so hard," he said as he approached the counter, shoving his fists into the pockets of his jeans. "Bear trapped in a cupboard, I guess you could say."

Words. You're supposed to say words, Blair, I told myself. "It's no problem." I tried to smile back, but it was probably a grimace.

He looked at the potions hovering in mid-air, then faced me again, that somewhat smile in place. "It looks like your magic caught them all. Good reaction time." When I said nothing—like an idiot—he cleared his throat and shifted on his feet. "Witch, then?"

In a way, it was frowned upon to ask other beings, '*What are you?*' but I wasn't offended. Mostly because I was horribly curious as to what mythical race this man might be.

"Witch," I confirmed when I found my sandpaper tongue.

He pointed to his head. "Dread Monster."

I almost gasped. "Male Dread Monsters are extremely rare..." I breathed without thinking. That explained the wrap around his hair and said hair's...heft.

Dread Monsters have deadly vipers for hair in their typical form, and those vipers turn anything they look at to stone. Usually, Dreads are women. When they have a male baby, the child is almost always of a different race, taking after the non-Dread-Monster father. On very rare occasions, a Dread mother will produce a male baby, but no pairing of *two* Dread Monsters had ever produced a male child—that we knew of.

"Sorry. I'm sorry," I fumbled with the words, shaking my head. But he bypassed it, unbothered.

"I'm supposed to be opening a café next door in a couple of weeks, and that Winslow guy has been riding my tail about city codes and red tape and—" He stopped and ran a palm over the scruff of his chin before he shoved his hand back in his pocket.

"Being a general menace?" I finished for him.

This elicited a huffed laugh from him and I hoped my face hadn't gone red—like Bill Winslow's.

"Yeah. If it's not him, it's that skinny guy that follows him around like a hyper chihuahua."

"Marcus. Yeah, he's less menace and more mouse. He's a Hobgoblin."

"Makes sense." He adjusted the collar on the button-down shirt he had open over a plain tee. "Listen, I don't mean to bother you, but Winslow won't let me put in my oven because he says there is a spell interfering with that wall and I could, quote, '*burn down the town.*'"

"Do you need help detecting it or something?" I asked, not following why he was in my shop. Not that I was exactly complaining...

"It's uh"—he pointed at my glowing stone hearth—"that wall."

"Ohhh," I dragged the short word out too far. "I see."

"Can you fix it?"

Not in a way Bill Winslow would approve of. "Sure. I just need to see your side of the wall." I didn't. It would certainly make it easier, but, c'mon. No one had seen inside the new café yet except the construction crew guys—who are far from gossips—and, apparently, the mayor and his little shadow.

"Right. Of course. Is now okay?"

"Sure."

I followed him out onto the sidewalk and he stopped so suddenly I almost ran into him.

"Sorry," I said, righting myself. "Sorry."

With a look of confusion on his face, he pointed at the apothecary. "Don't you need to lock the door?"

I snorted. "You're new here?" Obviously, Blair. Good thinking.

He sort of winced in a half-embarrassed, self-deprecating way. "Not used to small-town living yet."

"The construction has been in the works for moons," I

said as we walked the few feet from my shop to the café, "but I haven't seen you around before."

"I just arrived in Gloam Hollow a few days ago. I managed most things with the construction crew via video calls until my condo sold and I could finally move."

I wanted to ask where he moved from, but he was already opening the door and ushering me inside. The windows had been papered and taped to keep out prying eyes—not that Ms. Lilly Tuttle and Pepper Cornish hadn't camped out in front to sneak a peek every time the construction crew opened the door. I had no idea what I'd been expecting, but it was not the rustic industrial vibe I was seeing.

The walls were old, exposed brick, probably the original that had sat dormant underneath decades of plaster and sheetrock. Floors of deep, dark wood ended at a counter at the back made of black, sleek tile and boasting a shiny wooden bartop. Above it were four lanterns hanging from the tall ceiling—taller than mine—bronze globes with little specks of transparent gold that made the lights look like stars. In front of the counter was a line of black iron stools. Several tables were littered around the café, all different sizes and styles, yet cohesive shades of wood. Many of the tables and even the shelves behind the bartop still had sheets over them as a couple of painters moved around with brushes, but it was easy to picture the final product.

"This place looks incredible."

He actually smiled this time. "Thanks. This way."

"What did you name it?" It seemed to me he was awfully close to opening day not to have a sign up yet.

"I haven't decided."

I followed as he led me behind the checkout counter

and through a door that swung open to the kitchen. Immediately, I was assaulted by sawing, hammering, eight levels of dust, and almost a dozen workers buzzing about. Two big burly guys narrowly missed slamming into me, and they would have if—hey, I haven't learned this Dread Monster's name yet—hadn't grabbed me by the waist and hauled me out of the way.

"Thanks," I muttered awkwardly, brushing off my skirt and *really* wishing I'd put on my cardigan.

"Yeah." He cleared his throat. "No problem. The wall is just over this way."

Mr. Dread pointed in the direction of a blank wall that, logistically, would be the other side of my magical fireplace. Compared to the rest of the café, even the unfinished parts, the wall was boring. Untouched. We went to stand in front of it, and I marveled at my handy work—the fact my simple spell could render this side of the wall untouchable.

Not too shabby, if I do say so myself.

"Yikes," I murmured. "Sorry about that."

He shrugged, those fists in his pockets again. "Can you fix it? I need to get this wall ready for my oven delivery tomorrow."

All it took was a conscious effort to pull back a little of the spell. A pushing forward, rather, containing it mostly to my side of the wall. When I was finished, a thought struck me, and my lips quirked to the side.

"What is it?" Nameless Dread asked, his thick, dark brows furrowed.

"If I tell you what I have to do next, you can't tell Bill."

"Bill?"

"Winslow. The mayor."

I barely caught the hint of a wry smile from the corner of my eye. "Yeah, sure. Mum's the word."

"See, the thing is, I have to protect your side of the wall from my magical fire. Or poof—" I mimed an explosion. "But if I do that, you won't be able to do much with the wall unless I…"

"Unless you…"

"Combine two spells."

"And that's…bad?"

"Bad news!" came a voice from behind us, and I jumped.

Clutching my heart, I saw the resident ghost that had driven every other business out of this particular building. "Hi, Henry." I took a peek to see if Mr. Dread over there could see him.

He was most definitely staring at Henry's gossamer form, no small amount of ire showing in the set of his jaw. "You know this annoying ghost?" he asked me, glaring at Henry.

"I do." I smiled at Henry, who was, as always, dressed in a vintage suit, complete with a hat. He'd been a Gargoyle in life but died in his *person* form and that is how he remained. It was rumored that Henry had been the ah, decorative sort of Gargoyle, rather than the fierce kind.

Henry swirled away, distracted by something.

"Two spells are bad?" Mr. Dread got back to business.

I shifted on my feet to face him. "It is strictly forbidden regarding a historic building."

His green eyes narrowed as one side of his mouth tipped up. "Why do I get the feeling there's a really good story there."

"Oh, there is a very good story there. Maybe I'll tell you one day. If you're lucky."

I turned back to the wall, my eyes bulging. Was I *flirting*? When was the last time I'd flirted? The pickings are *slim* in The Hollow. Shaking my head to dislodge the cobwebs on that side of my brain, I concentrated on the delicate binding of spells. When I was finished, I brushed my hands together as if dusting them off after a hard day's work.

"Should I be worried about the combined spells if it's, you know, forbidden?"

"Only if a Tuttle Witch cast it." I looked at him very seriously. "Beware the Tuttles." He looked genuinely concerned and I laughed. "They're more gossipmongers than anything else."

"That can be just as dangerous," he mumbled. "Thanks for doing this, eh... What was your name?"

"Blair." I held out my hand for him to shake.

"Aramis."

"Not a problem, Aramis. Piece of cake."

Aramis jumped a bit and clapped his hands together, startling me. "Speaking of cake..."

And he ran away. Well, *ran* isn't quite right. His legs are so long he sort of...took three steps and was across the kitchen and back out in the dining area. He hadn't been even close to as animated the entire time we'd been talking and I wasn't sure what to make of it. I was still fumbling with minor surprise when he backed his way into the kitchen with two pastry boxes in hand.

"Pick a pie."

"*Pick a pie*. No sweeter words have ever been spoken." I was surely almost visibly drooling and Aramis chuckled. "Are you serious?"

"Very. You spell my wall"—he lifted one shoulder—"I give you a pie. It's the *small-town* thing to do, isn't it?"

I laughed, a full laugh. "Not in this town. We in Gloam Hollow know better than to invoke the wrath of the town baker. Did you actually make these?"

He looked a bit affronted. "I did. Obviously not here, with the lack of oven and everything. I had to try out which ones I want to offer on the menu."

"Don't let Minerva at *Toil & Truffle* know you plan to sell these."

"Beware the Tuttles?"

I chuckled. "No, she's not a Tuttle." I reached for the one marked *Death by Chocolate*. "Dark name for a pie."

"Well, it's to die for, as they say."

CHAPTER 4

The rest of the day at the apothecary was fairly uneventful.

When I returned from the café, I set the chocolate pie from Aramis in the mini-fridge in my workroom and made a deal with myself. I could have a slice once I finished brewing Mrs. Winslow's Dragon Tulip potion. Then, I would have some lunch and brew Anon's anxiety elixir. If there was still time, I'd whip something up for my Aunt Millie's sore feet she'd been complaining about.

The events went exactly as planned, a rare feat in life, and Aramis was correct. The chocolate pie was delicious. I thought I would die eating it, it was so good. How could a man that manly make a pie so tasty?

I know, I know, rotten Blair for making gender stereotypes. But it was more like the idea that it's completely unfair for beautiful women to also be funny or masters in the arts. It's not a fair shake for the rest of us regular folk.

Regular *magic* folk, as it were.

I was groaning over how tasty my second piece of the pie

was, leaning over the counter and shoveling it in my face like an Ogre when the door opened. Anon stepped in, a gust of chilly wind and a skittering of leaves following him.

"The season has officially shifted," he said by way of greeting.

I beamed, reaching under the counter to pull out my oversized sweater. I slipped my arms in and sighed. *Bliss.* "Your potion is there on the pick-up table," I said, gesturing with my thumb and walking past Anon to peer out the window. Yep, all the trees in the square and all the others I could see were russet and crimson, gold and cinnamon.

Hopefully, this season would choose to stick around a while, the leaves falling, dancing on the wind, gathering in piles but the trees never quite running out.

"Town Council will have the Harvest Festival date in no time," I mused, watching a gold and brown leaf swirl to the ground.

"What do I owe you for this?" Anon asked, holding the little glass vial up to the light of one of the gas lamps.

"Same as last time."

I'd looked up the last time Anon was in—four moon cycles ago. The vial was only good for about a moon's worth and I wondered why he'd taken so long to request more. Many of my patrons knew enough about medicinal herbs or possessed enough magic to handle most things on their own nowadays, what with the Magical Interweb that came out a while back. But there were some things that needed a personal touch, and some people preferred that hometown feeling of local artisans.

I assumed Anon was managing his stress and anxiety on his own for the last few moons, but he still just seemed extra frazzled. No one was there but us, so I decided to ask after him again while he fished in his pocket, dropping two to three loose moonstones at a time on the counter until there were enough.

"Are you sure everything is alright, Anon?" I swiped the stones into my hand and deposited them in the register.

Anon didn't look up, gaze firmly planted on his canvas high tops. "Things are fine, Blair." There was a shortness to his tone I'd never heard from him before. "Thanks. See ya.'"

He dropped the elixir back into one of the canvas *Copper Cauldron* bags I use for all my customers and hurried out.

Mrs. Windslow bustled in about an hour later, happy as a clam for her potion.

"Three drops on each bloom morning and night," I instructed, and she left.

By mid-afternoon, I'd narrowly avoided another piece of pie, written a grocery list, read four chapters of four different books next to the fire, and drummed my fingers on the counter for far too long. The only other thing I could do at this point was clean and I'd simply rather not. Besides, I quite liked Moss, the spider up in the corner behind the counter.

Time to close up, then.

I slung my bag over my shoulder, locked up, and stepped out into the crisp, *delightful* air.

If I hurried, I would have enough time to stop by Maureen McDuggan's and water her fish—yes, water her fish—grab what I need from the grocers, and still have enough time to run home and change from my sandals into boots—*Boots, I say!*—before book club.

Maureen lives in a small but sweet house just two streets off the square from the apothecary, so I took a left and meandered that way. Fish successfully watered and house firmly shut up (I did close a few windows she'd left open, unaware the drop in temperature would arrive), I made my way back toward the center of town.

I'll not lie to you, I skirted the square, avoiding *Toil & Truffle*. If my mom came close enough, she'd smell Aramis's pie on me with her Witchy senses, and we didn't need a dead Dread on our hands.

I popped into *Goodman's Grocery* and picked up one of the little hand baskets. Moseying down the aisles trying to recall what I needed—guess who left her list on the apothecary counter—I traded niceties with a few people and one ghost. His name is Bartholomew and he's either scary as all get out or the nicest gentleman you've ever encountered.

"Having a good day there, Bart?" I said as he eyed the fresh okra.

"Oh, it's a good one, Miss Blair. Just a right jolly day. I'm gathering the goodies for a picnic for me and Halsey." He grinned and I tried not to look manic. This was a telltale sign Bart would be intolerable for the next few days because Halsey had moved on to the afterlife and Bart would soon discover that. Yet again.

"Hey, why don't you let Halsey rest today and you go out and enjoy the music in the square, hm?" I mean, it was worth a shot...

"Halsey will love the music! I'll set up the picnic there!"

Uh-oh.

Bart floated off and through the front wall. Oh, well. He'd forget again soon enough and not everyone could see Bartholomew, anyway. We'd just have to be spooked senseless a few times a day for a while.

Pens!

That was one of the things on the list. I picked up a box of glitter pens. (Hey, there's no age limit for glitter pens.) Grabbed a few little snacks for book club, and the only other thing I could recall from the list: shampoo.

After checking out, I noticed there was a massive line all the way out the door of *Stonewood* and down the sidewalk.

"Lacuna has her pumpkin spice and ginger treacle menu up!" Cordelia Adams squealed at me as she rushed by to hop in line.

There was much cursing and shoving and general dispute because the Faerie cut in line to stand by Katarina, purple and blue Pixie dust mingling and settling at their feet.

Lacuna has the most divine autumnal drinks, but I didn't have time to wait in line, so I planned to just make some pour-over at home. I walked past, trying not to let anyone hold me up with small talk. Alas, Katarina caught my arm.

"Hey, I went by the apothecary a while ago but you were closed," she said.

"Ah, sorry, Kat. I forgot you were going to come by for that statement. I need to run these home." I lifted my market bags. "Can I give you the statement at book club? You'll be there tonight, yeah?"

"Sure, B. No problem!" She smiled and turned back to her animated conversation with Cordelia.

The next person to grab my arm and tug was Ms. Lilly Tuttle. "Blair!" she sang, crushing me and my market bags in a hug. This was normal, expected behavior from the older Witch, and she held the hug long enough that I knew what was coming next—the meddling. "Did you see that new boy in town?" she whispered in my ear. I was sure to have bright red lipstick smudges on my earlobe.

She finally let go. Well, she pushed me backward, holding onto my forearms.

"I assume you mean Aramis, the café owner."

Ms. Lilly gasped. "Is that his name?"

She fanned herself and I laughed. I knew she'd start peppering me with questions that weren't mine to answer, so I kissed her cheek—Ha! Gave *her* a *Vampiric Plum* lip print —and headed for home. Judging by the big clock in the square, I only had an hour to get to the inn for book club. Maeve, speaking of Vampires, did not like tardiness.

Back at the cottage, the trees were *breathtaking*. I gave myself a brief moment of joy to take in the picturesque scene and listen to the owls in the branches whisper their good evenings to one another—and one squabble up in an oak tree. The sun was already beginning to set with the abrupt change in season, and it was time for them to begin their night.

Maggie would be upset about the sun setting early. And that is exactly what she was griping about when I went inside and began to feed the cats.

"Blair, I'm meant for sun and sea and flowers!" She sat on the counter, running a hand through her curls and making them stick up all over her head. "Not this *sun going down before teatime* nonsense!"

I scratched Beetle behind the ears and stood from the cat bowls. "I know, Mags." My cousins were beautiful, dark, and slender—Maggie—and nerdy-handsome, olive, and lithe—Hamish. They took after their fathers, basking in the glow of the sun with ease, while I got to be the cousin who took after the Wardwells. We typical Wardwells are *not* 'sunny, hot days' kind of Witches.

I washed my hands and set some water to boil, listening

to Maggie rant as I measured coffee grounds into the brown paper filter. I nodded along and *mmhmm*'d when necessary. It was best to just let Mags get it all out.

When the kettle sang, I poured the water over the grounds, basking in my version of the sun—the aroma of coffee and the sound of it dripping into the glass pot. I grinned to myself and Maggie laughed.

"The Season of the Witch for you, isn't it?"

"I couldn't have said it better myself. I like to think I have a direct connection to our Autumnal Lady of Magic."

Mags hopped down from the counter, her many necklaces tinkling together with the movement. "I think you're right about that, B. Have fun at book club," she said as she headed upstairs and I poured coffee into my favorite mug—black with gold leaves on it.

"Hey!" I shouted when I thought of something, the coffee sloshing over the lip of the mug and burning my hand. I was shaking it out when Maggie stuck her head over the stair railing.

"Yeah?"

"I thought you had to work late at the salon. The whole dinner debacle with Hamish?"

Maggie made a horrendous face. "You won't tell him, will you?"

"Margaret Wardwell!" I shouted, but she'd already vanished.

Debating whether I should do just that and tell Hamish so *she* could fight with him for once, I lugged my coffee upstairs and set it on my vanity. I kicked my sandals into the corner, earning a hiss from the cat I did not know was curled up over there.

"There is food downstairs, Albis."

Let the heathens feast, he meowed softly, turning away from me. *Hamish gave me salmon earlier.*

I rolled my eyes and padded into my closet to dig out a pair of boots. Let's be real, I brought out two pairs. I put one from each pair on each foot and compared them. Both black, one with a chunky sole, one with a heel and pointed toe. Definitely the chunky ones paired with the skirt and sweater.

Satisfied, I checked the time and gulped down all the scorching coffee I could manage before rushing downstairs and into the night. The inn was only a short walk from my cottage, but it was a steep walk, as it rests at the top of Hollow Hill.

There it sat, a Gothic architectural masterpiece backlit by the moon—*Moonrise Manor Inn*. All sharp edges and spires, baroque woodwork and glowing windows.

Usually, most of us in Gloam Hollow refrain from using our powers too often, whatever they may be. It's not that we can't or shouldn't, it just...gets a little boring. Hiking up the hill to my grandmother's inn, however, gets old. So I transported myself from the bottom of Hollow Hill right up to the door and banged the knocker.

CHAPTER 5

I didn't wait for anyone to answer the door to *Moonrise Manor*. I only slam the knocker because, quite frankly, it's fun.

"Maeve! Grandma!" I called out as I kicked the heavy door shut with my foot, balancing a stack of books and the market bag of snacks in my arms. "I come bearing cheese puffs and sweet chili chips."

"In here, darling!" I heard my grandmother's voice call from the parlor.

Grandma Wardwell—along with her friend and employee, Tina, a Werewolf—was bustling about, setting up trays of cheese and fruit and at least six bottles of wine. It was far too much for the small group of us, but she still sets out a spread every meeting. Every once in a while, someone would bring a friend, or one of the inn's guests would come down for book club, but it was rare.

"Hi dear," Tina chirped. "We have a guest tonight!" She was beaming, so I assumed it was her guest.

"Color me intrigued," I humored her, setting down my

armful of books on a side table. "And who might this mystery guest be?"

Wine glasses *tinked* together as Tina lined them up on the sideboard atop a lace runner my Great-Great Grandmother Wardwell had made. "You'll just have to wait and see."

Grandma made a *pfft* sound and paused her rearranging of snack platters. "It's not me meddling this time," she told me. "Just remember that." I opened my mouth to object to any sort of meddling, but Grandma spoke again. "What have you got in that *Goodman's* bag?"

I handed over my junk food contribution and walked the perimeter of the parlor, looking at all the photographs along the walls. Some were of our family many, many generations back, others were old and grainy of different places in The Hollow, and some were of past guests, who preferred to have their time at *Moonrise Manor Inn* immortalized by a photo rather than a signature in a guestbook.

"Where is Maeve?" I asked when I'd made a full round of the room and she hadn't yet shown. Everyone was due to arrive in about five minutes and, as I've mentioned, Maeve is not one for tardiness.

"Oh, *banana's foster!*" Grandma cursed in her not-cursing-at-all way. "I forgot she went out back to get some wood for a nice fire. Be a dear and go help her, Blair."

I refrained from mentioning that the incredibly strong and tough *Vampire* Maeve did not need my assistance, and headed toward the back door.

On my way, I ran into three guests. One pair in the library—an incredibly sweet Troll couple. And one relaxing on the back porch in a rocker, a cup of steaming cider in hand. As soon as I saw the book in his lap, my stomach flipped.

"You must be Tina's guest," I said cheerfully, though I didn't feel it.

"Ah," he said with a nice enough grin, but it made me want to cringe. "I am indeed. Are you Blair, Lacuna, Maeve, or Katarina?"

My suspicions were evidently completely founded. "Blair. And you are?" *The next contestant on Meddling Elders!* I answered for him in my head in my best game show announcer voice.

"Apparently, I'm the prize bull about to be auctioned off to the highest bidder," he joked.

Alright, he's not so bad. Not classically handsome, yet easy enough on the eyes.

"But you can just call me Andrew."

"It's nice to meet you, Andrew. If you want, I can tell them you had an emergency and needed to leave." I meant to help the poor guy out, but it came out ruder than I intended.

He chuckled lightly and stood, the vacated chair still rocking. Hmm. Tall, too. I couldn't tell exactly without asking, but I thought he might be a Centaur. "It's okay. I already read the book." He held up his copy of *She Did It*.

"Don't say I didn't try then," I said teasingly, but I meant it. This guy had no idea what he was about to be subjected to. Especially if my Aunt Moira shows up. She hadn't been to book club in a while, but if Tina or Grandma told her this guy was coming, she'd be here with bells on. "I'll see you inside, then." I waved awkwardly and hopped down the stairs toward the deliciously foggy and autumnal treeline.

Maeve was there, ax in hand, but she was just sitting on

a felled tree staring at her motorcycle boots. "Hey, buddy," I said cautiously. "What's with the face?"

Maeve is, like most Vampires, stunning in ways that resemble classic art or marble sculptures. She is long and lean, with a short, sleek black bob that is asymmetrical and somehow makes her canines look even sharper. Her chin too. Perpetually in black, she is what you might call both a classic Vampire and a classic motorcyclist. Her boyfriend, Tom—a Werewolf and Tina's grandson—owns the tattoo shop off Peach.

Magical species do mingle, but we don't know a lot about the logistics of it. No one can really explain how it works. What we do know is, should separate species mate, biology selects one species or the other for a child, never a monster mix.

I shivered just thinking about the result of that. That would be, as my grandmother might say, *stranger than a pickle tree.*

Watching Maeve's face, I was struck by the thought of why Tina, as Tom's grandma, would be trying to potentially set Maeve up with Andrew.

"I'm going to hazard a guess here and say this general gloominess has to do with Andrew up there on the porch."

Maeve's ruby-red lips pursed. "You guessed correctly. I don't know what Tina is up to. Does she not want *me* with Tom anymore?" Maeve's shoulders sagged even more. "Or maybe she's mad at Tom and trying to get under his skin?"

Knowing Tom—and Tina—it was probably the latter. "Tina adores you, Maeve."

When Maeve and I were in school, Hamish, Maggie, and I were expected to work at the inn with her and Tina. In many ways, Maeve was the granddaughter Tina didn't have.

Maeve's piercing blue eyes flashed. "You're right. She does love me. So what did Tom do?"

Uh-oh. This might be worse.

"How about we put the ax down and just come inside? Club is about to begin, and there's a nice, big glass of wine in it for you."

Maeve mumbled a half-hearted protest but rose. Although Vampires prefer blood, they've evolved enough to get what they need from raw and lightly cooked meat. Aside from that, wine is their main food group, even though they can partake of whatever they'd like.

I started to follow Maeve up to the inn but remembered the wood for the fire and stacked a few logs. I let my magic carry them to the manor, floating behind me until they settled nicely in the hearth of the parlor.

Grandma flicked a bit of magic into the hearth and a fire roared to life as I sat in a floral wingback chair. "It's tiiiime," she sang. "Grab a drink and a plate and let's get started."

I planned to let everyone else go first, pulling out my battered copy of *She Did It* to look over my notes and annotations.

"I can't believe you desecrate books like that," Maeve sneered playfully, clearly in a better mood. For now.

"I can't believe you won't even crack a spine," I shot back. "Books are meant to be read, felt, *held*, not treated like breakable relics."

"Yeah, yeah." She plopped down crookedly in the chair next to mine, kicking one leg over the arm as she popped a piece of cheese in her mouth.

"Hey, ladies," Lacuna took a seat on Maeve's other side. I considered warning her that her choice of seat might lead to

Andrew sitting next to her but refrained. Maybe she'd want to sit next to the handsome guest.

"I didn't think you'd make it, Lac," I said instead. "What with that gargantuan line outside your shop this afternoon."

Lacuna laughed and took a sip of white wine. "Anon took over for me after we ran out. He'll close up tonight," she said, looking around. "Where's Katarina?"

"Late as usual," Maeve sniped. She wasn't wrong.

"Did Kat get anything off your fall menu before you ran out?" I asked. "I saw her in line a bit ago."

"Yeah, she was one of the last few." Lacuna grinned at me and lifted her chin. "I did bring a canteen of some maple coffee." She winked at me. "Just for you."

"Yes!" I stood in a rush, my book falling to the ground. "That. Immediately."

Maeve picked up my *poor, helpless book* as I made my way to the table. As I opened the canteen and inhaled the scent of perfection inside, Grandma clapped her hands sharply.

"Let's get started!" Everyone shifted to look in her direction in front of the fire and at our guest. "First, I'd like to introduce you to Tina's guest. All, this is Andrew." Murmured hellos ensued, and Andrew strolled over to sit next to Lacuna as predicted.

With coffee poured into a delicate china cup patterned with dark florals and one trial sip taken, I piled my little matching plate with fruit, cheese, and a few of the chili chips I'd brought.

As I did this, Grandma had already begun asking everyone's suggestions for our next read. "I brought a few of my choices!" I called, pointing with a toothpick at the stack of books on the side table.

It was closest to Andrew, so he read off the titles. Tina

took notes as everyone gave suggestions, and I returned to my seat. Once that was finished, Grandma began her line of questioning regarding *She Did It* which always led to a lively, fun debate and, more often than not, a deep conversation.

I *love* book club nights.

Snacks eaten, I pulled my knees up to my chest and cuddled down into my sweater, sipping my coffee and listening to everyone chat. Andrew, quite surprisingly, contributed a great deal to the conversation. We rarely selected fluffy or overly feminine books—unless Katarina's choice won the draw—but many of the themes in this read were *real* feminine issues. Andrew, it appeared on the outside, was quite the feminist.

"It's a simple fact, regardless of mythical race, women don't feel safe around men. Period," Andrew said animatedly, his hands moving as he spoke. "I think the author does an excellent job of showing that. I mean, our main character is a fierce Orc and she still feels unsafe walking alone at night. There's a deeper issue here."

Lacuna and Maeve both blinked at him and I almost spit out my coffee. I reached out and kicked Maeve's boot, my expression screaming: *Remember TOM?* because she was practically drooling. Maeve flashed her fangs at me and I hid a smirk behind my cup.

Tina was eyeing all of us with a sly grin. Grandma was prodding Andrew with more questions, I assume to test his stance. I don't know what would have come of it, because Katarina crashed into the room then.

"Something's happened!" She was breathing hard, Pixie dust swirling around her in a purple cloud.

I immediately rose, rushing across the parlor and discarding my cup sloppily on the table. "What's going on?"

"I was on my way up the hill and I got a call from a source about a news story, but I couldn't make out what he was saying, the reception is strange on the hill." She was beginning to babble, so I put a hand on her arm. That seemed to settle her enough to keep going. "I called him back as soon as I got to the inn, and he said someone has been attacked!"

"*Attacked*?" we all said at once.

"Attacked?" I asked more calmly. "In The Hollow?"

Katarina nodded, a mad gleam in her eye that seemed part fear and part exhilaration. I would be lying if I said I didn't feel both as well. Nothing ever happened in Gloam Hollow...

"In the park," Kat explained. "That's all I know. I have to go!"

"Take Blair!" Grandma shouted at the fine mist of Pixie dust where Kat had been. "She's a good little snoop!"

I shot a glare at Grandma as I snatched up my bag, but she wasn't wrong. "Let me know what the next book pick is!" I called over my shoulder as I ran out after Kat.

CHAPTER 6

"Wait!" I called after Kat outside the inn.

She stopped long enough to pull on a jean jacket over her cream turtleneck and strappy mini dress. "This is strange, right?" Her eyes were still wide and shifty, but they certainly hadn't lost their frenzied glint, either. "Let's go! I don't want to miss anything."

When we neared Dew Park, I hauled her under a street lamp, grateful that I'd changed from sandals to boots. "Slow down. Are we just charging in or observing unseen?" I asked, our breaths fogging the air between us.

"I'm the press. I'll flash my badge and we can waltz right into the action."

Somehow, I doubted it would be that easy. "I'm not the press, though." And *very* unwilling to miss the action. "I can't do a concealment spell, either, because Sheriff Oliphant can see through most of those." Though, not usually a Wardwell spell, but I didn't feel inclined to mention that part to Kat.

"I'll say you're with me." Kat shrugged, her earlier fright

completely drowned out by excitement. I wanted my trepidation squashed, too, but the fact remained that someone was hurt. I couldn't, in good conscience, grab hold of the thrilling side of things.

Before I could respond, Kat took off again. It wasn't long before we reached the park, a gaggle of people huddled together around a bench. I could make out Sheriff Oliphant's distinct silhouette under the lamppost's light, but the rest were too close and jumbled together to make out who they were.

I had a sudden urge to phone my mom. She sometimes walked the scenic route through the park on her way home to the inn. I, however, had an aversion to portable phones and most handheld devices thanks to an unfortunate incident of butt dialing when they first came out. Never again.

Surely, Sheriff Oliphant would have phoned Grandma at the inn if Mom had been attacked, so I shook that fear loose.

Katarina and I strolled up to the small crowd like we belonged there. One of the shadowy figures broke from the group and marched over, scowling at us. "Oh, brother," Katarina sighed. "Here it comes."

"*What* do the two of you think you're doing here?" Bill Winslow reprimanded.

"We're the press, Bill," Katarina shot back.

"The last thing we need is news of this spreading."

"The people deserve to know what happens in their town. It's their right as free citizens of Gloam Hollow." Yikes. I thought she was laying it on a bit thick, but I didn't say as much. "Now get out of our way."

I let them continue arguing and snuck away,

approaching the crowd quietly. Ask forgiveness, not permission, right?

A man named Ronnie stepped to the side and I peered past several sets of shoulders to see one of the town paramedics, Carla I think her name is, on one knee, tending to none other than Anon. My pulse spiked and before I could think, I was pushing past people and approaching the bench.

"Anon! Are you alright? What's happened?"

Anon's lips formed a thin line, and Sheriff Oliphant stepped up. "Now, Blair, I know he's your friend, darlin', but this is serious police business and Anon here isn't to speak to anyone about it quite yet."

I looked, bewildered, from our kindly sheriff to frazzled Anon, but he wouldn't meet my eye. "Yeah. Okay," I said mechanically and pushed back through the people that were left watching.

"Folks, everybody needs to leave the premises immediately," the sheriff was saying, but my head was buzzing and I barely heard him.

Anon attacked? In Gloam Hollow. It didn't sit right. I had a sinking feeling Anon might be mixed up in something he shouldn't be, but how I knew that or what exactly it could be, I had no idea.

"Hey," Kat said as she jogged up. "Did you learn anything? Bill and Sheriff Oliphant won't let me anywhere close."

"It's Anon." My voice was wooden, and Kat gasped. "I mean, he seemed okay. There was a fair amount of blood on his shirt but the paramedic was only looking at a wound above his eyebrow. Head wounds bleed a lot," I rambled.

"And he was cradling his arm. I think it was bent at the wrong angle..."

"Wow." Kat blanched. "You got all that? You were only over there a few seconds."

I really had noticed a lot, pinpointed important things... An unwelcome sense of pride flooded me, but I was ashamed of thinking about it while Anon was hurt. Possibly in danger.

"Kat." I pulled her to a stop at the edge of the park—it seemed I had to do that a lot. A scattering of whispering people passed us. "We have to figure out what happened to him."

"Of course!" she said with a bounce, and I got that sinking feeling again. "This will be the first big news break for *The Gloam Reporter!*"

"This isn't some story, Kat," I snapped. "My friend is *hurt*. Someone hurt him."

Kat gaped at me. I don't think I'd ever been so short with her before, but I was rattled. Beyond rattled. "I need to clear my head," I exhaled and walked away.

The night had grown far chillier than expected, and I wrapped my arms around my chest, snuggling into my sweater as I walked down an alley onto the square. I didn't really know where I was going, and it never crossed my mind that Anon's attacker could be out there somewhere posing a threat.

Something with Anon just didn't feel right. Didn't add up. He was always on edge, sure, but today it had been much more pronounced. And didn't Lacuna say he was closing up *Stonewood* for her so she could go to book club? I lifted my oversized sleeve to see my dainty watch and paused dead in my tracks. *Stonewood* wasn't supposed to close for another twenty minutes. I looked across the square in the direction of the coffee shop. Sure enough, there was no rectangular glow from the window.

Disconcerted, I decided to walk the square's perimeter to see if there was anything out of place. Maybe stop in the bakery afterward and see if Mom left any good donuts behind.

As I passed Art's candy shop, I peeked in at all the little souvenirs lined up under the security light. It wasn't exactly rare to have tourists in Gloam Hollow, but it was most common in the cold season when there was fresh snow on the mountains and our resident dragon snuggled in her cave until it was warm again. Hiking lower on the mountain was a treat, but not worth traveling to our tiny town. Once Draak Summit was vacant, now *that* was a sight worth traveling for.

Along this line of thinking, I considered if Grandma, Mom, or the Aunts had mentioned anything about more guests at the inn. I knew some of the café's construction crew was staying there, as they'd been hired out of town. I'd seen maybe a handful of new faces around the square, but none that just screamed: *I'm a threat!* Though, I suppose most threats don't paint themselves as one, or they'd never have any victims, now would they?

With that terrifying thought, I moved down the list. No one had told me where Andrew came from—if he was a guest at the inn or new to town. There was the elderly Troll couple staying at *Moonrise Manor*, but I doubted they could climb the stairs without huffing, let alone give Anon a run for his money.

The lights were still on at the café as I passed, and I wondered if the crew was still working or— A shadow passed by the concealed window and I jumped.

"*Sweet candy corn,*" I whispered to myself, clutching my chest." I was way too high-strung.

I chuckled at my jumpiness if only to convince myself it was safe out and I had nothing to worry about. I'm a Witch, after all. But there are certainly some creatures much stronger than me that go bump in the night. Still, I turned around and went in the other direction, back toward the bakery.

As I was passing the apothecary, all closed up safely, I froze, a realization striking me—jarring me more than I wanted to admit.

Aramis was also new to Gloam Hollow.

I quickened my pace toward *Toil & Truffle,* and spelled open the door, shutting it firmly behind me and throwing the bolt. It was dark inside and I didn't bother to switch on the lights. Instead, I conjured a golden orb of magic and let it dance around me to light the way.

"Mama," I called, not expecting an answer. "It's me. Are you in?"

Silence.

I strode to the phone they use to take orders and rang the inn. Maeve answered on the fourth ring. "*Moonrise Manor Inn*, this is Maeve."

"Maeve, it's me."

"Hey." Her voice sounded closer like she'd put her hand up to shield her mouth as she talked into the phone. "Did you guys figure anything out? We've been on pins and needles over here."

"It was Anon," I said.

"Goddess!" Maeve sucked in a breath. "Is he okay?"

"He seems to be just banged up a bit. He was attacked in the park, but Sheriff Oliphant won't let him talk about it. I came to the bakery to see if Mom was still here but it was empty. Is she there?"

"Yeah, yeah. She got in shortly after you left. She's been worried sick. I'll tell her you're alright. Are you coming here or going home?"

"I think I'll head home. I need to check on Mags and Hamish."

"Right, of course. I'll relay the message."

"Thanks, Maeve. You're the best."

"I know." And she hung up.

I returned the phone to its hook and made to leave, but then I remembered the morning's donut debacle and went to the back to see if Mom had left anything good. Usually, she would drop off extras at the end of the day to the school, but they weren't back in session yet.

"*Yesss.*" I found two whole trays of delicacies wrapped in cellophane and mine for the picking. I grabbed a bakery box and lifted the wrapping as carefully as I could. (No one wants to wrestle with cling wrap any more than they have to.) I filled the box to the brim with donuts, truffles, croissants, muffins, and cookies, and closed the cellophane. This would be the *perfect* peace offering for Hamish.

I ensured everything was how it looked when I arrived and made my way toward the front door. I was just about to unlock it and step out when I heard a thud and a groan from outside. Heart pounding, I extinguished my magic light and hid between the windows so I could try and move the shade —see what was going on out there.

There was another thud and a sickening gurgle sound. I stopped breathing. Too scared to move. Too terrified to look. *What* had just happened out there?

I heard footsteps racing away on the sidewalk and conjured every iota of courage to peek out the window.

My heart lodged in my throat. A *body* was crumpled on the street in front of *Toil & Truffle*, a dark puddle slowly spreading beneath it.

Pulling air into my lungs as best I could, I unlocked the front door with trembling fingers and ran outside. When I got closer, it was so much worse. I dropped the bakery box, that hand coming up to cover my mouth. And then I removed it and started yelling. "HELP! SOMEBODY HELP!"

Across the corner, the front door of the café almost flew off its hinges as Aramis came running out. "What is it?" He started for me but halted when he saw the body. "Are you alright? What happened?"

"C–Call the sheriff!" I commanded, then lost my mind completely. He could still be alive. I had to check. I had no business looking for a pulse on the person, but someone had to.

I sank to my knees as Aramis shouted to one of his workers to call a paramedic. I told him it had to be Sheriff Oliphant and he relayed the message to someone behind him.

Then, he was next to me in a second, pushing my trembling hands away gently. "Let me do this." Without rolling the body over or touching it more than he had to, he pressed two fingers to the man's jugular.

"Aramis," my voice was so quiet, "I–I think he's dead."

One look from the Dread Monster told me I was correct.

CHAPTER 7

Mrs. Cobblepot shuffled into a small seating area of the ramshackle Gloam Hollow Sheriff's Department. She was carrying a silver tea service tray, but everything was rattling and sloshing and Aramis jumped up to take it from her.

"Thank you kindly, dear," Mrs. Cobblepot said as Aramis set it down on the table between our chairs. "You're such a nice boy."

Many, many thoughts had been coursing through my mind for the last three hours since seeing the body. None of them were coherent and most were borderline insane. Added to that clump of unhinged thoughts was now the loudest of them: nice men who bake pies and help elderly ladies carry tea can't be murderers, right?

"Sheriff Oliphant should be back any minute now," Mrs. Cobblepot said. But she'd been saying that for over an hour.

My leg would not stop bouncing where I sat hiding in my sweater. But at least the trembling had stopped.

Aramis, still standing, poured a cup of tea and handed it to me. "Drink. The warmth will help your nerves."

When I glanced up, he was looking pointedly at my bouncy leg and I made it still. Hey, small success! His fingers brushed mine as he handed me the cup and the leg took off again. "*Son of a gingerbread man,*" I hissed to myself.

"Pardon?" Aramis returned to his seat next to mine.

"Nothing." Why was he so *calm* about all of this? Because he's a murderer? Have I really been left in this building with a murderer and only Mrs. Cobblepot to save me?

"You know," Aramis said, glancing around the office that more resembled an old lady's sitting room, "when the sheriff said he was bringing us in for questioning, this is not what I pictured."

Why? Because he'd been behind bars before? *Get a grip, Blair.* "Coziness is next to gospel in Gloam Hollow," I said, proud of the almost-evenness of my voice.

Aramis was quiet, so I risked a glance at him and he was staring at me intently. "Did— Do you think you knew him?" he finally asked.

The question had the opposite effect I thought it would have. Instead of troubling me, it grounded me. Facts. My leg stopped bouncing. "I'm not sure," I answered. "I didn't get a good look. I didn't recognize his outfit or anything. It was fairly plain—jeans and a green shirt. I did notice he had a tattoo on his left arm, though. A sparrow I think it was. Small. Not something I recall anyone around here having. We have a tattoo parlor here, but that sparrow wasn't Tom's or any of the other artists' style, so I assume he wasn't from around here or didn't wear short sleeves often enough for me to notice that tattoo." When I finally stopped talking,

Aramis's brows were knit together in the middle and he was sitting very still. "Um." I looked at my teacup. "Sorry for rambling."

I took a long sip of tea, relishing the warmth as it slid into my belly. He was right, it did calm me. Until I realized he hadn't said anything and was still staring at me looking almost angry.

"You apologize too much," he finally said, his tone gravelly, something like a growl.

"Excuse me?"

He slid his forearms down his thighs, leaning over and lacing his fingers. "You apologized to me multiple times earlier today. Then, you apologized to not only a dead body for accidentally brushing his pants with your boot, but also to the paramedic for your squished pastry box that was nowhere near her, *and* to Mrs. Cobblepot when she held the door for you." He shook his head and huffed a laugh. "The last one doesn't even make sense. And now you've gone and apologized to me for *talking*. A very astute speech, I might add."

I blinked at the possible-murderer-slash-Dread-Monster.

"You have just as much right to exist and speak your mind as anyone else," he went on. "And, frankly, most abuse their freedom and say stupid things, not detective-level observations after only being with a victim for a few minutes." His green eyes bore into me, and I realized they were almost twin shades to mine. "Stop apologizing, Blair."

I couldn't have responded if I'd wanted to. In fact, I probably would have apologized for apologizing so much. Thankfully, Sheriff Oliphant charged in then, all business but still as fatherly as ever.

"Blair, Aramis." He sat hard in a chair across from us, not bothering to call us into his tiny office. We were the only ones in the building aside from Mrs. Cobblepot, who seemed to be snoring in the breakroom. "I'm going to need to hear the events of tonight from both of you." He looked from me to Aramis. "Separately. Blair, why don't you go on home." Sheriff Oliphant reached to the seat next to him and picked up my bent and crumpled pastry box, handing it to me. "Deputy Pete will take you. I'll come by the cottage in the morning."

I took the box and stood, but suddenly felt like I didn't want to leave Aramis alone to be questioned.

Something in my face must have given me away, because he smiled at me, just a small uptick of the corners of his mouth. "I'll be fine. Get some sleep."

When I turned to Sheriff Oliphant, he was glaring at Aramis. "Is this not evidence?" I held up the pastry box lamely.

"No, sweetheart," the sheriff said. "Take it on home before there's another Donut Disaster at the cottage." He winked at me and I almost bent to kiss his cheek before I recalled why we were there. He was not my father, but he'd been the one to step in and take care of Mom and me after my dad left. He will always have a special place in my heart.

"Goodnight, then," I said to them both and left.

Deputy Pete jumped up from the curb when I walked outside into the cool night and tipped the cowboy hat he loves to wear toward me. "Miss Blair, I'll drive you home."

I smiled. Pete always acted like he lived in the wrong era and the wrong location, but it was a place of his own making where ladies were precious and men chivalrous. "Thanks, Pete, but I think I'd rather walk."

"Oh. No, no ma'am, I'm sorry, I don't think I can do that," Pete stammered and I could see what Aramis meant about apologizing too much. "Sheriff'll have my hide."

"Just tell him it was my choice."

He was still gaping at me like a fish when I walked off.

It seemed like I should be scared to walk all the way home alone, but I wasn't. Aramis had given me a lot to think about and it calmed me. I truly didn't think I knew the victim and that, in conjunction with Anon's attack, was more than disconcerting, but it made me think something specific was going on. And I wanted to find out what it was.

Still jittery despite how exhausted I felt, the walk home was short and uneventful. Beetle met me at the door, meowing as if she had never in all her days been fed. I wasn't listening intently enough to see if that *was* what she was saying, but probably. I scratched her behind the ears and wandered into the kitchen.

Maggie's fork clattered to her plate and she and Hamish both rushed me. I could only make out bits of: *are you okay?, a dead body!, what happened?*, before they shoved me into a chair.

Maggie went to serve me a plate of the pasta Hamish—I assumed—had made and I slid the sad pastry box across to him. "Truce?"

Hamish frowned at me but opened it. "Is there any blood on these?"

I snorted. "Shouldn't you two have eaten hours ago? It's got to be...what?"

"About three in the morning," Hamish answered, shoveling a truffle in his mouth and talking around it. "*Somebody* lied about having to work late so she wouldn't have to cook dinner." He narrowed his eyes at Maggie, who giggled. "By the time we finished arguing over it, Aunt Minerva had called and told us what happened. You should probably call her."

I rose to do just that from the landline, not having much appetite anyway and wondering if I shouldn't have gone by the inn on my way home. She's probably worried senseless.

It was a correct assessment. By the time I convinced Mom she didn't need to come over in the middle of the night and got off the phone, Hamish was falling asleep in his food.

"Hamish." I pushed his shoulder and he snorted awake. "Go up to bed."

"I wanted to hear the story!" he complained sleepily.

"It can wait for morning. I'm going to go to sleep too." I looked at Maggie. "Meet for breakfast in a few hours?"

She nodded. "I'll just clear the plates."

I pulled Hamish up from his chair and we climbed the stairs to our rooms.

Aramis

The fatherly mask Sheriff Oliphant wore with Blair vanished the moment the door closed behind her. He was staring at me like I was the worst kind of monster.

I leaned back in my chair, knees apart and arms crossed. I knew all too well how this went.

And I would not be the first to speak.

Finally, Oliphant did. "I take it you're going to sing me the old 'wrong place, wrong time' song."

I smiled at him and felt my dreads flicker into vipers underneath my head wrap. "Right place, right time."

He rested his elbows on his knees. "Listen, I'm as happy as the next guy that we're getting a proper café in The Hollow, and I've heard nothing but good things about you, but you have to meet me halfway here."

"Then you probably shouldn't have walked in here thinking I'm the killer or I'm planning to abduct Blair, who you clearly feel protective over."

Oliphant chewed on the inside of his cheek. I could tell because his mustache twitched. I couldn't pinpoint exactly his race. Gentle but tough when necessary. Griffen maybe. If not, probably Warlock.

"Why were you and Miss Wardwell out so late?" he finally asked, redirecting the conversation.

Wardwell, huh? All that talk about Wardwell and Tuttle and Blair hadn't mentioned that she's one of them. Intriguing.

"Answer the question, Hawthorne," the sheriff barked at me.

I sighed. Small-town cops, I swear. "I don't know what *Miss Wardwell* was doing, aside from the fact she was outside the bakery with a bakery box. And, unlike you, I didn't look in it while she was distracted."

Oliphant's jaw ticked. He probably thought he was sly opening it to check the contents when she'd left it on the back of his cruiser to talk to the paramedic.

"I, on the other hand, was in my café trying to finish the kitchen so I can install the oven that's set to arrive in"—I looked at my watch—"five hours."

I watched his eyes drop to my feet, assessing my story.

"If the dust and paint on my boots aren't enough, you

can ask the two construction workers who were with me." I knew he already had. Any cop worth his salt would have.

"Alright." He leaned back in his chair, mirroring me. "You're inside the café. Then what?"

"I heard someone screaming for help, and I ran outside. That's when I saw Blair and then the body."

His head cocked to one side, as I expected it to. "You saw Blair *before* the body? Wasn't it between you and her on the sidewalk?"

Good catch. "Yes, but I think we both know Blair can draw an eye."

Oliphant coughed. Is Blair his daughter? Niece? There's some sort of relationship there. She almost looked like she was going to give him a kiss on the cheek before she left, then thought better of it.

I spread my hands, palms up. "Look, she was screaming, and it all happened quickly. At first, I thought the lump on the ground might be her jacket or a bag she dropped before my brain caught up with my eyes."

"Go on. You saw Blair, then the body."

"She told me to call you, but she was headed for the body. Shaking."

"Wait. Headed for the body? What do you mean?"

"She knelt beside him like she was going to check for a pulse, but I told her I'd do it. That's—" I shook my head. "That's not something she should have had to deal with."

"So you checked for a pulse?"

"Yes. I shouted for one of my guys to call the paramedics and Blair insisted he call you. I assumed paramedics and Sheriff come as a package deal around here or something. Then, I confirmed there was no pulse."

"And what happened between that time and when the paramedics and I arrived?"

"Mostly Blair trembling. She apologized to the victim once, for her boot accidentally brushing his pants. I ran into the café to get her a glass of water, but, again, this is a small town. By the time I came back out onto the sidewalk, you were already pulling up."

Oliphant studied me for a long time, but I kept still. "That's it?" he finally said.

"That's it."

"Did you know him—the victim?"

"No." My pulse kicked, like a lie. But it was the truth. Or something close to it.

CHAPTER 8

Blair

When I came downstairs the next morning feeling like a train wreck, I found my mom in the kitchen frying up bacon and eggs. Instantly, the tightness in my chest loosened.

"Hi, Mama."

"Morning, Pumpkin Pie," she chirped, but I could tell she was worried. "Don't you look cute!"

Muddled head or not, my outfit *was* pretty perfect. Dark plaid mini-skirt, black tights, oversized knit sweater. "Thanks," I said as I slid onto a stool at the kitchen island.

Mom passed me a steaming cup of coffee in my favorite Jack-O-Lantern mug and turned back to the stove. "Are you ready to talk about it?"

Was I? "I don't know. I think you know about as much as I do. I assume Corbin called you?"

I watched Mom's head nod. From behind, she didn't look

much different than me. Not that I ever saw myself from behind, but you catch my drift.

Corbin Oliphant had always carried a torch for Mom since they dated back in their teenage years. I think that's why he's never married. But Mom claims she's happy not being tied down. She always says she has all she needs in herself, me, her sisters, and her mom. I do, however, have my sneaking suspicions that she does give in every once in a while to the sheriff's wiles. And really, who could blame her? He's kind, and a looker in his own way with salted-gold hair and scruff, bright blue eyes, and just enough meat on his bones to be considered fit but not ridiculously toned. *Dad bod*, Mags called it. Plus, he was a powerful Warlock. Powerful enough to see through *most* of the other magic in town—Wardwell and Tuttle excluded. Hence why he was made Sheriff.

I curled my hands around the pumpkin mug, letting the heat seep through the knitting of my sweater, the sleeves too long and covering most of my palms. The warmth settled my heart like Mom's presence. Like the sip of tea that Aramis had insisted I take last night for that very purpose.

I tossed thoughts of the Dread Monster away. "Did Aunt Millie open the bakery today?"

Mom sent her magic, a spray of glittering teal, to begin washing the dishes in the sink. What Maggie had left of last night's pasta mess, by the looks of it.

"Moira did. Once she scared Deputy Pete off and ripped down the crime scene tape." Mom shook her head and I laughed. That sounded just like Aunt Moira. "Millie had a forest excursion planned for the inn guests this morning. Moira wants to get the boutique open by midmorning, though, so I'll need to finish up here and run over to the bakery."

Aunt Moira is a force to be reckoned with. Hamish's mom and the Gloam Hollow fashion queen. As the owner of *Spellbound Boutique*, Moira is always dressed to the hilt. Aunt Millie, however, is her polar opposite in personality. (All three sisters have that Wardwell red hair in different shades). Mildred Wardwell is eccentric like her sisters but in all the ways of flora, soil, and *being one with nature*. She runs a flower shop called *Broom & Blossom* that doubles as a community garden. Her shop provides all the fresh flowers for the inn she, Mom, and Moira technically own with Grandma. And Millie often takes groups of tourists—when we have them—into the woods around Gloam Hollow to explore. I would say Mags fell very far from her mother's branch of the Wardwell tree. You couldn't pay her to spend five minutes in nature.

"Has anyone heard from Anon?" I asked Mom, sipping my coffee. "Mm, you added nutmeg to this."

"Nutmeg and a calming spell." She winced apologetically over her shoulder.

I chuckled at her meddling, mother-hen ways. "Well, I needed it. That's for sure."

She laid the bacon on a pumpkin plate that matched my mug and set it on the counter in front of me. Maggie shuffled down the stairs then, her hair a silvery hurricane around her head.

"Morning, sunshine," I said and Mags groaned something, rubbing at her eyes.

"Coffee," she grunted. "Please."

Mom laughed. "Coming right up." She shoved the bacon

plate closer and I dug in, starving after missing dinner last night. As she made a cup of coffee for Maggie, she informed us that Anon had been taken to the nearest hospital to be checked out, but as far as she knew, he'd returned early this morning and was banged up but fine, resting at home.

Hamish had come down halfway through the recap and was munching on a piece of bacon standing next to my stool. "Does he not remember what happened?"

It seemed Hamish and I had similar suspicions about that.

"Corbin says the boy claims he didn't see anything. He was struck from behind and tackled to the ground, his arm twisted behind him," Mom explained.

"Okay, so he was mugged?" I asked for clarification.

"That wasn't mentioned."

I exchanged a look with Hamish. That seemed to wake Maggie up, too, or maybe she'd just finally had enough coffee. "Then why attack?" she put in.

"And why weren't his glasses broken?" I added.

Hamish gave me an impressed nod of approval. "You've got a point there," he said, reaching for another piece of bacon.

"Now, you three stop and think for a moment," Mom censured, hands on her hips. "Why are you acting like this poor boy is lying? Isn't he a friend of yours?"

"Yes, Auntie," Hamish said, "but he's been so odd lately."

I smacked Hamish's arm. "You noticed that, too?"

"He came into the library the other day asking for the strangest books. I mean, he always looks up pretty peculiar stuff, but this was weird even for him."

"What did he want books about?" Maggie asked.

"I don't remember exactly..."

My knees cracked as I stood—a cool life development. "Will you see what you can find out? Get me a list or something of the titles he checked out?"

"I guess so, yeah..."

"Thanks." I took one last sip of coffee. "I need to go check on Lacuna. I'll come by the library this afternoon."

"Isn't Corbin coming by this morning?" Mom asked.

I'd completely forgotten. "Just send him to the apothecary if he does."

"Blair–"

"What about me?" Maggie jumped in, looking like an excited puppy. "What's my job?"

"Go see what Katarina has dug up about the whole ordeal."

"Woah, woah, woah." Mom put her hands up. "Just wait one minute. This is a leap, even for the three of you. What is this? Playing detective out of the blue?"

"Someone is attacking people in our sleepy little town," I said. "We can't just sit by and do nothing."

"That's what the police are for!" she argued, her voice loud enough that her magic at the sink startled and dropped a plate. "*Police*, Blair."

"All two of them?" Hamish snorted, mouth full of eggs.

I pulled up a foot, resting it against my opposite calf like a flamingo, hip against the counter. "I love Sheriff Oliphant as much as anyone in this town, but his biggest case to date was uncovering the *heinous* graffiti artist of six years ago."

Mom frowned, but I knew I'd gotten her there. We'd spent too many nights playfully mocking how frazzled everyone was over a cartoon hotdog-man graffitied on the side of Bill's office building. The culprit had been none other than Tom, resident tattoo artist. He'd spent a night in 'jail' for his crimes, being fed biscuits and gravy by Mrs. Cobblepot before Sheriff Oliphant made him scrub all the graffiti off by hand.

Remembering that debacle with Tom gave me another brilliant idea I kept to myself.

"Not to mention Deputy Pete..." Maggie added to the police debate.

I pointed a finger at Mags. "That, too. They need all the help they can get."

A good old-fashioned Wardwell Battle of Wills ensued as my mom and I stared at one another. Finally, Mom's eyes narrowed. "You listen here and you listen well. If you're going to do this, you better not get caught and you better be certain you're doing it for the right reasons." She let her words hover like a threat. "Not just because you want to absolve a handsome Dread Monster that just came to town."

Mags and Hamish turned to me in unison. "*What* now?" Mags pressed, almost giddy with the prospect of juicy gossip. I don't know where Mom got that information from, be she might as well have dangled a raw steak in front of a Vamp. Best to get out now.

I went around the island and kissed Mom on the cheek. "Thanks for breakfast. Would you consider taking a basket of baked goods to Anon's house?" I didn't think he'd be truthful with me after the way he avoided my questions yesterday. But Mom? She was hard to resist.

She eyed me suspiciously. "To spy on him?"

"Yep. See what you can find out with your motherly charm." I wiggled my shoulder at her with a grin.

She frowned at me, but I was fairly sure she'd do it. Witches are naturally curious and charmingly sneaky. Especially Wardwells.

"What are you going to do after you check on Lacuna?" Mom asked cautiously.

"I'm going to figure out if there's a connection between the two attacks." In a bigger city, maybe they wouldn't be connected. But in Gloam Hollow? Something wicked was afoot.

I think my mother was offering up ancient prayers of protection when I walked out of the cottage. By lunchtime, she would probably have four wards cast around me and sneak a protection potion in my afternoon coffee. Gotta love her.

The first morning walk of official autumn was divine. Leaves trickling ahead of me with each step, crisp air in my lungs. There is nothing better than cozy sweaters, tights, and the promise of magical pumpkins sure to crop up around town at any moment.

I was even excited to investigate the happenings going on in The Hollow. It gave me something much better to do than pass the time in my empty apothecary.

Even so, there was still that tinge of unease in my stomach and the frightful image of the victim when I closed my eyes. Part of me toyed with the idea that I should be *more* unnerved by it. Realistically, though, all I truly saw was a person crumpled on the ground and a dark puddle.

Perhaps this was one of those things that would hit me later, PTSD-style.

Or maybe I'm just a rotten person.

Kicking an acorn down the sidewalk as I approached the square, I settled on drawing the Sneak Attack of PTSD straw, rather than the I'm A Terrible Person one.

Stonewood was absolutely packed with people. Some of them were probably the regular crowd I narrowly missed each morning by coming in early, but many were shuffling in to ask after Anon and see who knew what about the murder. Bill Winslow might have wanted to keep the happenings of the prior night quiet, but nothing could be kept secret in Gloam Hollow, and there was zero chance Katarina hadn't written about it on her blog.

I squeezed past a few people headed for the counter, but I saw *The Hollow Herald* newspaper over Ms. Lilly Tuttle's shoulder. Right there on the front page: BODY FOUND OUTSIDE TOIL & TRUFFLE BAKERY

"I guess Bill couldn't stop Warren from printing the news any more than he could stop Kat, hm?" I said as I sat down opposite Ms. Lilly.

She folded the newspaper over her chest, appearing scandalized. "Oh, honey, you know how this town is." Leaning in, she looked around the busy coffee shop and whispered, "I heard you found the body. Was it gruesome?"

I knew Ms. Lilly would never ask something so boring as, '*Are you alright?*' "I think I missed all the gruesome bits."

"I also heard that hunk of a man who just got into town was with you." She raised her drawn-on eyebrows suggestively.

"Aramis," I said with a chuckle. "He's the one we talked about yesterday who is opening the café. And we were not *together*. I screamed, and he came running out."

Ms. Lilly fanned herself with the paper. "Dreamboat behavior 101. I'm glad someone finally figured out who was opening the café. That's been the mid-level mystery of the year around here."

Ms. Lilly was right. We all saw the SOLD sign go up several moons ago, then watched the construction crew arrive and heard the news it was a café, but until yesterday, none of us had known who was opening it. Not even Kat or Warren from *The Hollow Herald*. Bill must have known—probably was the one who sold him the building—but the rest of us had been in the dark until he arrived, which is not an easy feat here.

"Well, Ms. Lilly," I said, standing and pushing in the chair, "keep your ear to the ground. Let me know if you hear anything good."

"Oh, of course, dear. We both know I've already sent gathering spells out." We both also knew she meant *gossip*-gathering spells. Ms. Lilly stuck her nose back in the newspaper and I made for the counter while the line was shorter.

Lacuna had awful bags under her eyes like deep bruises. "Lac, did you get any sleep?"

She smiled weakly at me. "Not much. Maeve took me on her bike out to the hospital to see Anon, but they'd already sent him home by the time we arrived."

"Have you seen him? How is he?"

Lacuna started making my usual autumn coffee order, talking as she worked. "No, I haven't. He and Tom have their house shut up like a battlement. They wouldn't even let Maeve in."

Things were just getting weirder and weirder...

"My mom said she was going to take a basket of goodies over there. I hope they at least let her drop it off." And she can get a peek at Anon.

Lacuna shook her head, a weariness draped over her. "I don't think they will."

I debated just wishing my friend a good day, telling her to let me know if she needed anything, but I didn't do that. "Lac, have you noticed Anon acting a little strange lately?"

She snapped the black plastic lid onto my to-go cup, her head tilted to one side. "Hmm. He was a bit on edge yesterday, but other than that he's seemed to be normal to me."

Lacuna was sweet as pie, but she was always distracted, her head in the clouds. I risked one more prodding question. "Hamish said he checked some odd books out of the library a while back. Do you know anything about that?"

She tucked a bit of her lilac hair behind her ear. "That was probably when he checked out books about the Mortal Lands for me."

My eyes widened a tick. "I didn't think that was strictly allowed."

"It's not." Lacuna lowered her voice. "Tom said he's getting this new tattoo ink, it *glows*."

I gasped, but lowered my voice, too. I didn't know what all Lacuna's tattoos meant, but I knew they were important and part of the reason she was always so distracted. I hadn't been able to deduce much more than that. "Lac, that's perfect! When do you go in?"

She shook her head and batted a hand dismissively. "You know Tom. He's hard to pin down."

A glowing tattoo on Lacuna's inky skin was going to be incredible. Wait... "Hang on, what does that have to do with the books Anon checked out of the library?"

"I wanted inspiration. For the tattoo. And Anon knows how much I love the Mortal Lands."

Color me intrigued. "Aren't those restricted? How did Anon get them out without Hamish throwing a fit?"

Lacuna grimaced. "I don't know. He said he had 'help' of some kind."

The man who was content not to speak to anyone for

days on end had an accomplice to help him check out books at the *library*? I flipped open the spout on my coffee lid and fished some moonstones out of my bag. "Thanks, Lac. Go easy today and let me know if you need anything."

"Thanks, babe. I'll let you know if I hear from Anon."

CHAPTER 9

Aramis

"Where did you get this oven from, Boss?" my employee, Steven, asked with a grunt as we shoved it into place. "It's a beast."

"Don't worry about it. And don't call me '*Boss*.'"

I'd told him that a dozen times since hiring him two days ago. My first Gloam Hollow employee. I'd been worried about hiring anyone from a small town, so I'd shipped in my own building crew, but now that the café was set to open in a couple of weeks, I had to start hiring wait staff. So far, I'd landed on Steven—Troll—and a quiet young Pixie named Kendall.

She told me she has a sister named Katarina who runs an online news blog and her dad is the principal at the local school. Steven said he moved to Gloam Hollow ten years ago after vacationing here to see the dragon on Draak Summit and falling in love with the town.

That was the extent of what I knew about my employees and I wasn't sure if that was preferable or terrifying.

Both, I guess.

Steven's side of the oven slammed against the wall and an iridescent shimmer like a mirage rippled up to the ceiling. I'd never seen magic quite like Blair Wardwell's and that was another thing I didn't know if it was preferable or terrifying.

Both, again, I guess.

"That'll do it," I said, dusting off my hands. "Go ahead and take five. The next project is hanging all the signage. Then you and Kendall can go get the menus laminated."

"Sure, Boss!" Steven trotted off and I sighed. I wouldn't have hired him if I'd known he had half the pep he did.

Grabbing a rag off the counter, I set to wiping down the oven and decided I would affectionately name it *Beast*. Shiny as it was going to get, I threw the rag over my shoulder and headed to my office.

The door was cracked and I stopped, listening. I knew with absolute certainty I closed it when I walked out. Light on my feet despite heavy work boots, I slunk forward before flinging open the door.

"Steven! What the hell are you doing in here? *Out!*"

Steven dropped everything he was holding and it spread all over the floor behind my desk. He scuttled out, blubbering apologies until I thought he might cry.

When he left, I slammed the door shut and rounded the desk to see what he'd been looking at. My heart sank when I realized it was just the signage I'd told him we would hang after his break. I pinched the bridge of my nose and held it for five breaths.

Blair

Sipping my coffee and enjoying the crisp walk toward the apothecary, I pondered what Lacuna had told me, but it was crowded out by a plethora of other thoughts.

I would pop in to check on the shop, make a few lists of what I knew so far, then I'd head to the library to see what Hamish had worked out. The books seemed harmless enough despite the fact they weren't supposed to be checked out, but it was still a lead I wanted to look into.

I was just about to pat myself on the back for sounding like a proper sleuth when I almost bowled into someone. "Oh!" I fumbled with my coffee but it tumbled to the ground with a splash.

"Aw, Blair, I'm sorry."

Steven Littlebottom bent down and retrieved the cup for me. He looked in it forlornly and dumped it upside down. "Not a drop left."

"No problem, Steven." I took the cup and tossed it in the nearest bin as he bent to pick up the lid that had popped off and tossed it in, too. "It's just coffee." I smiled at him, but he didn't return it. "Hey, are you okay?"

"I think I'm about to get fired."

"Fired? I didn't know you'd found a job, that's great!" Steven has a big personality and general difficulty holding down a job.

"Yeah, but I'm about to get fired. Boss caught me in his office and yelled at me."

"What were you doing in his office?"

"I was just doing what he'd said! That's all!"

That didn't sound like the store owners on the square to overreact like that. Well, maybe Bill, but his office was off Peach St. "Who is your boss, Steven?"

He threw a thumb in the direction of the café and I immediately saw red. "*Aramis* is your boss?" I spat.

Steven nodded.

Oh no no no sir. I stomped toward the door ready to barge in and give Aramis a piece of my mind, but he was coming out at the same time. We collided with an *oomph* and he caught me by the arms so I didn't lose my balance, instead half-carrying me out the door, unable to stop his trajectory.

"Morning," he said coolly when we were stable on the sidewalk.

I backed up one step, straightened my skirt, and pointed my finger at his chest. "Did you *shout* at Steven?"

His gaze slid from me to Steven then back. "I did." There was no contrition in his tone, only plain, simple fact.

"I don't know how you do things where you're from Mister Big City, but in Gloam Hollow we do not treat employees like that!"

"As a matter of fact," Aramis drawled, "I was coming out here to apologize." He flashed his teeth at me, then directed his attention to Steven, his face softening some. "Steven, I'm sorry. I thought you were snooping. I didn't realize you were just getting the posters that needed to be hung up."

Snooping, huh? What did this Dread Monster have to hide that warranted yelling at his employee for being in his office?

"It's alright," Steven said softly.

"It's not," Aramis countered. "What say we start over, and I'll even let you keep calling me '*Boss*'?"

Steven perked right up, nodding repeatedly. "You got it,

Boss!" He bustled past us, his usual hop back in his step, and disappeared into the café.

I glared at Aramis darkly, but he was looking at the brownish puddle next to my shoes. "Did you stumble upon another body, Wardwell?" He smirked at me and turned back toward the café.

I hadn't told him my last name so someone snitched. And he knew good and well that was *coffee* and not blood. Miffed, I started stomping toward the apothecary, but he called out.

"Hey, Wardwell."

Scowling, I turned around. "*What*, Dread Monster?"

"How about you apologize less when it's unnecessary, and I'll start apologizing more when it is."

The sudden sincerity in his green eyes pushed away a fraction of my anger. "Deal."

He smiled again, less snark with a hint of warmth, and walked into the café, leaving me to go begin my note-taking.

I threw my bag behind the apothecary counter and started rummaging for paper and a pen. I found one of Maggie's many tablets on a shelf and considered using it, but that sounded...terrible. Hand-written is always preferable if you ask me. Technology is more a curse than a blessing.

"Aha!" I snagged an almost-empty leather journal from under the counter and one of the new glitter gel pens from my bag—a deep purple.

I'd just written NOTES in a swooping script at the top when I heard a sound. My pulse hammered, but I was tired of all these little frights that were actually nothing.

"Who's there?" I called out, convincing myself this would *not* be the time that it was actually something dangerous.

Puck, little Puuuuck, a voice mewed, mimicking how I call out for the ginger cat. *Tis I, tis I. Who be there yonder?*

I'd given him one book of poetry. One.

I threw flames into the hearth and saw Puck sit up in one of the chairs and begin cleaning himself. "Why don't you talk like a poet when the other cats are around?"

He gave me a derisive sniff and curled up in the chair to sleep. I didn't even want to know how he made it to the shop. He'd probably made Hamish mad and he'd magicked Puck here before going to the library.

Shaking my head at my cat, I leaned on the counter and got back to my notes, slipping off my heeled wingtip shoes in the process.

- ANON ATTACKED
- UNKNOWN PERP
- GLASSES NOT BROKEN, DIDN'T SEE ANYTHING
- ANON HAS BEEN ACTING STRANGELY
- HAD AN ACCOMPLICE TO SNEAK THE MORTAL LANDS BOOKS OUT OF THE LIBRARY
- TOM HAS NEW GLOWING INK *IMPORTANT?
- ANON AND TOM WON'T LET ANYONE IN THE HOUSE
- UNKNOWN VICTIM KILLED OUTSIDE BAKERY
- NEW TO TOWN:

  - CAFÉ CONSTRUCTION CREW
  - ANDREW (INN)
  - VICTIM (POSSIBLY)
  - ARAMIS

Frustrated that was all I had, I wiggled the pen in my hand rapidly as it clicked against the counter. Eventually, I slammed it down and left the apothecary. I don't have a phone, but the bakery does.

Nearing the corner, I made to step down onto the *empty* street but saw Bill up the sidewalk and thought better of it. Unfortunately, he still walk-jogged over.

"Blair, there is a Town Meeting tonight. 7 p.m. Be there." He glanced down at my shoeless feet and rolled his eyes back into his head. "Please wear *shoes*, Miss Wardwell."

"I have tights on," I muttered like an insolent teenager.

"Wait! Is this about the murder?" I shouted after him, but Bill had sped away faster than I thought he could move. He stopped long enough to turn around and scowl at me, but then he was on his not-so-merry way.

I shrugged and walked into the bakery, happy to see my aunt was still in. "Hi, Auntie," I chimed along with the entry bell.

"Pumpkin Bug!" Moira glided over and smashed me in a hug before stepping back to admire my outfit, per usual. "This look is giving—" She stepped further back and eyed me, one finger tapping her chin. "Dark academia," she finished.

"Ding, ding, ding. Just missing my lovely wingtips."

Moira made a chef's kiss sound. "Perfection. I should add a line to the boutique, shouldn't I? Or do you do all your shopping on that"—she waved a hand flippantly, disgust written on her poised features—"Interweb thing?"

A laugh popped out of me. "Gross."

Moira shifted to stand next to me and bumped my hip with hers. "Agreed." Her heels clicked as she went back behind the display case and grabbed her purse. "Your mother should be here any minute, but I've got to run. Will you hold down the fort until she gets here?"

"Sure. I need to use the phone, anyway."

"Perfect. Thank you!"

"Oh, hey," I said before she could get out the door. "Bill says there's a Town Meeting tonight. Is it about the murder?"

Moira's face soured. "Don't busy your mind with that mess, dear. I think Lilly said the meeting is about the Harvest Festival. See you later!"

The door shut behind her and I picked up the phone, in a hurry before the next wave of bakery patrons came in. First things first, I dialed Maggie's cellphone. She picked up on the first ring—typical. "Mags. What did you learn from Katarina?"

I heard Kat's high voice in the background say, '*heyyyy girrrrl*,' before Maggie spoke. "We're getting some brunch at *Tin Melon*, so it's loud."

Seeing as *Tin Melon* is the only place to get real food at this time of day until the café opens, it's a hotspot as much as *Stonewood* is. "No problem. What did you guys figure out?"

"So far not a lot. No one wants to talk to Kat more than speculation. Nobody seems to know anything about the victim or Anon's attacker. If they do, they're not talking. Do you have any more info on what the victim looked like or anything?"

I did have the description I gave Aramis last night, but... I didn't want Kat too involved, not after her reaction at the park. I didn't want this to be just some story, some way to amp up her blogging career. Anything Kat publishes could be seen by anyone, anywhere. That gave me an idea and I sucked in a breath.

"Mags, I have to go. Talk later!"

I slammed down the phone and rushed to the door,

forgetting I was supposed to be keeping the bakery open until Mom returned. "Bah!"

Alright, fine. Regroup. I spun on my heel and went back to the phone to dial Sheriff Oliphant's office. Mrs. Cobblepot answered just as Mom came through the door of the bakery, three customers filing in behind her. She shooed me away and I took the phone off the wall, headed to the kitchen as far as the cord would stretch.

"Yes, Mrs. Cobblepot, it's Blair Wardwell. Can I talk to Sheriff Oliphant?"

True to her character, Mrs. Cobblepot did not place me on hold, nor cover the phone with her hand, so I heard her arguing with the sheriff. I stuck a spoon in a near-empty frosting bowl and licked at the sweet glob while I listened. He didn't want to take the call because I hadn't kept our appointment for this morning and now he was late somewhere. She thought he *should talk to the nice Wardwell girl. What would Minerva think if he didn't answer the phone for her daughter?* That got him to the phone and cleared up a few old suspicions of mine along the way.

"Sheriff Oliphant." His voice was clipped, but it made me want to giggle.

"Hiya, Sheriff, it's Blair."

"You didn't meet me at your cottage this morning. We had things to discuss."

"I really told you everything I saw already, but I have some questions for you."

There was a small pause, and I pictured Mrs. Cobblepot urging him to talk by winding her crepe paper hand around and around. "What can I do for ya', darlin'?"

"I wanted to see if you had any more information yet

about Anon's attack or the murder victim and his attacker. Do you think they're the same person?"

"Now, Blair. Don't get mixed up in all this. I'm sorry you were there to witness any of it, but you don't need to worry. I'm taking care of it."

Hmm. How to make him cave... I put on my best sad-girl voice. And, yes, I felt a stab of guilt for it, but plunged on, anyway. "But the thing is I *did* see it. And I feel like I can't get it out of my head until I know the facts. When I close my eyes, I just see the body lying there and I don't know what happened or who he was... Did he have a family? A daughter like me?" Too far, Blair. Too far.

"Okay, alright," Sheriff Oliphant cut me off at the same time I cut myself off. "I need to know that if I tell you what happened to the man, it isn't going to make things worse for you. Can you be sure of that?"

Not even a little bit. "Yes. Facts help me round out scenarios in my mind so they don't go wild." That part was true.

He let out a breath through his nose that made the line sound windy. "The victim died of four knife wounds. He would have survived if one of the incisions had not been to his lungs."

"What a way to go," I breathed, not having to fake the intensity in my voice. "Any leads on who might have done it?"

"Not yet, I'm afraid." He coughed. "Look, Blair, I need to go. We're still investigating and there is a lot of ground to cover."

"Sure, just one last thing. Could you tell me his name? The victim?"

"Blair." There was warning in his voice.

"I just–" I stammered, not faking it. "I just need to have a name for the man. What if he was still breathing when I first got out there? What if I could have saved him?"

"Don't do that to yourself, darlin'. Only misery lies down the road of what ifs."

My heart gave a little pang. Sheriff Corbin Oliphant was a good man—Warlock, as it were. "Just a name, Corbin, and I can let it rest. Please?" Truth, truth, lie.

He let out a sigh of all sighs. "We don't have a name. He was an out-of-towner and is unidentified at this point. A John Doe." As if he knew I would find thirteen more questions to ask (and I had) he said, "*Bup bup bup.* No more questions. And do not breathe a word about any of this to *anyone.* Most of all Anon Bishop."

"Wh–what? Why not Anon?" But the line was already dead.

Sheriff Oliphant suspected there was a connection, too.

"Blair Wardwell," Mom censured playfully when she entered the bakery kitchen.

I sat quietly, still in shock over what Sheriff Oliphant had told me on the phone

"Are you in your stockings with frosting on your nose?" Shaking her head but laughing, she tossed me a rag. "You'd think you were four years old again."

Though she was joking, I did make a mental note not to forget things like my shoes if I'm to be a proper sleuth. "Did you get to see Anon?" I asked, wiping the frosting remnants off my face.

"Sort of, but there's no time to talk about it now." She grabbed a giant tray of brownies. "Get the door for me, will you?" I hopped to open it, pressing her for details until she sighed. "I have a line of customers out there. We can talk more later, but I say trust your gut. Witches have a strong sense and intuition is half the battle, Pumpkin."

She was through the swinging door and I narrowly escaped it smacking me in the face. I decided to sneak out the back to avoid the rush of patrons and possibly scope out the alley for clues.

Alley was a city term that did not really apply in Gloam Hollow. They were all just glorified sidewalks, doubling as narrow streets lined with quaint houses. Behind *Toil & Truffle* was no different.

The bakery door shut behind me and I stood surveying the scene. A lovely buttercream house sat directly between the bakery and Art's candy shop, boasting a white picket fence and loads of wisteria. Next door, a cozy gray house with a wrap-around porch peeked out behind a few large oak trees ablaze with autumnal hues.

I sighed. Investigating a murder in a town with homes like these was ludicrous.

Considering said murder had taken place in front of the bakery and there was no quick getaway except through the square and down a side street, it was probably a wasted effort to look back here, anyway.

I started off around Art's *Gloam Hollow Candy and Souvenir Shop* back toward the apothecary, but my intuition sparked. I reminded myself to thank Mom for the Witch Sense reminder and darted back behind the bakery with cold toes. I also reminded myself to get my darn shoes back on.

Standing there staring at the yellow and gray houses, hands on my hips, I listened inwardly to that Witch sense.

Moments later, I growled. Nothing.

Maybe there was a spell I could use.

"Wait!" I shouted to myself, startling a bird out of a maple tree. The park where Anon was attacked sat just behind this row of houses. I rushed to the far side of the yellow house. *There* was a little pathway to the right that could only lead to the park.

Eight shades of giddy, I practically ran to the back door of the apothecary. (Except, on principle, I do not *run*.) If I was going on a clue hunt, I at least needed my shoes on. It wouldn't hurt to have the aid of a tracking spell, either.

When I spelled the back lock open, the door protested on its hinges. We hardly ever lock our front doors in Gloam Hollow during the day, let alone use back entrances. Speaking of, I didn't lock the door of the apothecary when I left. Perhaps I needed to start doing that with a murderer on the loose. The thought sent a shiver down my spine.

Sliding the deadbolt back into place, I made a beeline to my Not For Sale bookshelf. Rather than the mishmash of titles and genres available to customers, I also had a small shelf of spellbooks for personal use. I'd been known to let others borrow them from time to time, but, for the most part, they simply aided me in casting a spell or brewing a potion.

Puck meowed—very catlike—from his place in front of the fire as I ran my finger down the row of grimoires.

"There you have it." I plucked the tome off the shelf and carried it to the counter.

Flipping open a spellbook is a feeling I would never tire of. There is nothing like the scent of yellowed pages and ink, the lingering magic of old tickling your nose with the dust. Sometimes, I could even feel remnants of spells from as far back as six generations of Wardwell Witches. If scent and memory served correctly, the last time I'd used this particular grimoire was five moons ago to brew a strong fertility potion for Laura Simons. Who, I might add, is now *four* moons with child.

There were uses for my apothecary yet! I only needed to hang on and use my wits. Perhaps if this tracking spell was effective, Sheriff Oliphant would enlist my help in future cases. My fingers stilled over the pages. Surely there wouldn't *be* any more cases in our sleepy town, right?

I shook my thoughts loose. It was wishful thinking that the sheriff would want my help, anyway. But if he did, it would be to solve petty thefts and pranks gone wrong. I could live with that. It might even be fun.

Flipping through the spellbook was incredibly distracting. Within a few moments, I had an entire page of notes on spells and potions I wanted to try out later. Finally, I found exactly what I was looking for. "Aha!" I was saying as the bell above my door tinkled.

To my shock and possible dismay, Aramis strode in, his hands full.

"I come in peace and coffee." He held up a coffee cup and what looked to be a food container.

I narrowed my eyes at him but said nothing. Man, that coffee smelled good though. So did whatever he had in that to-go box...

Cautiously, as if I might be spooked like a horse, Aramis approached the counter and set the goods down in front of me. "Coffee since you spilled yours, and brunch because"— he shrugged—"I had to test out my new stove."

In an attempt not to seem too eager or let my guard down, I continued eyeing him sidelong, but I could tell all the ire had left my gaze. Wordlessly, I picked up the coffee cup and removed the lid to sniff its contents. "You named the café I see," I noted, studying the new logo: *Spectre Café*

"Had to settle on one sometime." He shrugged one shoulder. "Patty at the paper supply store printed a few different options I was deciding between on cups, and I liked this one best."

"The name fits. I like it. You picked the fancy spelling, too," I said simply before taking one tiny sip. "Holy gods." I almost groaned, "This is delicious. Do *not* let Lacuna taste this."

Aramis chuckled, a deep, velvety sound in his chest that I did not think helped my case against him. "Lacuna can't find out about my coffee and Minerva can't find out about my pies, hm?"

"Not unless you want a hex put on you."

"Well," he said, leaning over the counter. "I had a nice chat with Minerva *Wardwell* this morning when I took her a pie."

"You did *what*?" It wasn't until the words were out of my mouth that I realized he'd put two and two together about who Minerva was to me. "And yet you're still standing."

"Your mom is a lovely Witch," he said. "She did, however, make me sign a contract to sell her donuts in my café."

A laugh bubbled up out of me. "That sounds about right. She has one with Lacuna to stock her croissants."

"Smart woman."

"You won't be sorry. Her donuts are a bit of a national phenomenon. I'm pretty sure half the tourists come here just for those and her truffles."

"I don't doubt it. She gave me one of each this morning." Aramis straightened and took the liberty of opening the to-go *brunch* box. "Eggs benedict with a side of shredded hashbrowns and a container of a sauce you should consider drizzling on the benedict. It's a little out of the ordinary, but trust me."

Trust him. I wasn't so sure about that yet. Mom probably only had him sign that contract rather than fight him over dessert sales because she thought Sheriff Oliphant would run him out of town soon.

"What's in it?" I eyed him down my nose, sneaking glances at the *amazing*-looking food.

Watching my darting attention, he laughed. "The glaze is essentially ratatouille purée. It sounds strange, but it's really good." He lightly smacked his palm on the counter. "Ah, I forgot a fork."

"That's alright, I have a stash." I bent down to retrieve one from a shelf and when I popped back up, Aramis was looking at my crime notes from earlier.

"What have you got here?" he said casually.

My mouth fell open in horror, and I snatched the notes, almost stabbing him with my plastic fork. "None of your business!"

"You really shouldn't get involved in this murder stuff, Wardwell." All teasing had left his tone. "Seriously."

"*Trust you,* my foot," I muttered as I stored the notes in my bag.

This time, the hint of a chuckle in his voice returned. "*Curiosity.*" His smile was too disarming. "That's all it was."

"Curiosity killed the cat, you know," I shot back.

"Good thing I'm a Dread Monster, then." With a smirk, he strolled out of my apothecary with his hands in his pockets.

I stewed for two more minutes before the aroma of the food won me over. The first bite without his secret sauce was phenomenal, but once I drizzled the sauce on as he suggested, it was completely out of this world.

If he'd poisoned this meal, I was about to die a happy Witch.

Aramis

Going back would be stupid.

I told myself as much as I stood outside the café, debating like a schmuck.

Yes, definitely stupid to go back.

I walked into the café to find Steven rolling silverware at one end of the register counter and Kendall filling salt shakers at the other. She was talking to another Pixie sitting on a stool who had to be her sister. They were just about identical aside from the color of their hair, wings, and Pixie dust.

"Hiya, Boss!" Steven waved enthusiastically.

"Hey, Steven. Good work on the silverware. When you're done, will you call the produce guy and make sure he has everything we need in stock?"

"Sure thing, Boss!"

I clapped him on the shoulder. The kid was growing on me. "Good man."

"Hi!" the unexpected Pixie squealed at me and I nearly flinched. "I'm Katarina with *The Gloam Reporter!*" She bounced off her stool, Pixie dust scattering on my clean floor, and stuck out her hand.

Way, *way* too much bubbliness in this girl. Reluctantly, I took her hand and shook it. "Aramis. What can I do for you?"

I glanced at Kendall, making a mental note to tell her no

one but staff was to come in here without my permission before we opened. Hopefully, I wouldn't make her cry like I had Steven. Had that really been just this morning? I needed to get more sleep.

"Well"—she grinned from ear to pointed ear—"the café is opening in a couple of weeks and I wanted to interview you for my blog!"

Nightmare. A literal nightmare. "Uh, that sounds—" Terrible? Horrifying? "You know what?" I threw a thumb in the direction of the door. "I, uh, forgot something. Go ahead and interview Steven and Kendall here."

"Oh, I—"

But I was already back out on the street in four long strides.

I was just taking a breath, deciding where to hide, when I saw Blair come out of her shop. My feet were already headed toward her before I could stop them. "Hey."

She looked up, those big green eyes like orbs of magic behind her round glasses. "Hey, yourself."

Damn it. I'm gonna do it, aren't I? Inwardly, I sighed at myself, but outwardly, there went my mouth. "I have to test out the entire menu before opening. Why don't you come to the café on Starday night, and taste-test some more dishes?" My arm started moving erratically. "You know, maybe bring a couple of friends." I shoved my hand in my pocket to stop the flailing. "You could be my taste testers. Like a— Like a soft opening."

She blinked at me.

"Think of it as a truce. A white flag."

She smiled and a knot formed in my stomach. This was a terrible idea.

"Sure. Starday, around seven?"

"Yeah. Perfect," I confirmed, and she walked away.

CHAPTER 11

Blair

A soft opening of the café.

It didn't sound half-bad. As long as Aramis didn't plan to murder us all. Just in case, I'd make my plus-two Hamish and Maggie. Our powers wouldn't do a whole lot if Aramis removed his hair wrap and let his dreads turn into *dreaded* vipers to turn us all to stone, though.

My heeled wingtips clicked as I walked around the square and made a right on Lotus Street headed for the library. "Hmm," I hummed to myself. Maybe I could spell Aramis' hair wrap into place, unremovable—just to be safe.

Blessedly, no one stopped me on my trek and I climbed the steps to the stately Gloam Hollow Library. My day was shaping up nicely, indeed. A quick trip to talk to Hamish, then I could skip lunch since I had first and second breakfast. After that, I'd try out my tracking spell before the town meeting. I might even have time for some relaxation between those two agenda items. A nice tea, a book... Oh! That reminded me...

I scooted off to the side at the top of the steps and began a message to Mom. She knows my aversion to technology, so we worked out a lovely little spell that uses secret notes. I pulled out my spelled paper from my bag and a pink (Mom's favorite color) gel pen.

What book won the club draw?

I jotted down the note, then watched the ink begin to sparkle and lift from the paper. The greatest and trickiest part of the magic was that no one could see the messages once they left the spelled paper. It was spectacular.

I didn't expect to hear back for a bit, as it was nearly lunchtime and the bakery would be packed for hours still, but hopefully, I'd hear before I left the library and could pick up the new book for the month. Two birds, one stone. Except I'd never hit a bird with a stone—I'm not a monster.

Paper and pen stowed away, I heaved at the library door and waltzed in, inhaling the magnificent scent of *books*.

"Hey, that's a new sweater vest, isn't it?"

Hamish immediately shushed me when I walked up to the desk talking. So did a crotchety Gargoyle reading at the nearest table.

"Yeesh," I whispered. "You lot are irritable."

"It's a library, B."

"Fine. What did you find out about the books Anon checked out?"

He motioned me around the desk and we crowded in front of his computer. Anon's name came up on the screen followed by a list of books with mix-matched titles. "They're not actually all that strange," Hamish said. "It's just that they don't jive well. *Pickle Canning For Beginners, Live and Love Better, Adventure to Death Mountain*," Hamish rattled off the titles. "I suppose it just struck me as odd and I remembered it being more peculiar than it was."

They were definitely peculiar choices for Anon, though.

"Well, have I got some news for you." Head tilted to one side, I reconsidered. "Three pieces of news, actually, but two parts Maggie should be present for."

Call Hamish a nerd if you like, bookish and eccentric, but he *loves* news. "Do tell."

"It turns out"—I looked over at the Gargoyle in the face of a young lady who had shushed me when I came in, and put my back between her and Hamish—"that Anon actually checked out restricted books somehow."

Hamish stood up, almost toppling his wooden stool. "He did *what*?"

More shushing, this time from several readers.

I filled him in on all Lacuna had told me about the books. "We need to go look at the Mortal Lands section."

"He *didn't*... You have to have a key to get in there!" Muttering, Hamish marched off and returned a moment later with a ring of old skeleton keys I desperately wanted to hold.

When he stomped away, I jumped to follow down several gloomily lit rows of books taking so many twists and turns I didn't think I'd be able to make it back out on my own. Finally, we stopped in front of what I can only describe as a black iron cage. It was archaic and incredible.

The keys jingled together in Hamish's hand as he reached for the lock, but I grabbed his arm. "Can I do it?"

He looked at me like I was crazy.

"Please?"

With a roll of his eyes, he handed me the keyring and smoothed out his vest while I did the unlocking. The click of the gate opening was ultra-satisfying. I handed the keys back to Hamish and followed him inside.

"It has to stay dark to keep the books from fading," Hamish explained as he lit a small gaslamp that surely had a protection spell on it so it wouldn't, I don't know, catch the precious tomes on fire.

Each book also had the original dust jacket on it, as in a cloth covering to keep dust off. At the section marked *Mortal Lands* with a little bronze plate, Hamish began gently taking the cloth coverings off.

"What's that rattling sound?"

It was hard to see in the dim light, so I sent a globe of magic to hover over Hamish.

"Chains," he said, holding up one so I could see. "Magic chains. There is no way Anon came in here and got books without the key. Lacuna has to be mistaken."

He returned that book to its jacket and place, moving on to the next. When he pulled that cover off, he cursed in Grandma Wardwell fashion. "*Troll feet on a skunk!*"

I rushed over, my orb taking a dive to better show the title. *Pickle Canning for Beginners.* Exactly one of the titles checked out under Anon's name. "Decoy books."

By process of elimination, we found all the titles 'checked out' by Anon.

"Let's put them all back," I said when we were done and thoroughly flummoxed. "We don't want anyone coming back here and seeing empty spots."

Once the books were put away and the cage was securely locked again, Hamish pointed toward a set of comfy chairs.

"Let me go make sure someone is covering the desk and I'll be back."

I sat in one of the chairs, sighing at the comfort. I was used to walking quite a lot in Gloam Hollow, but this mayhem had made for extra steps today. A tiny *ding* sounded that only I could hear, and I looked up just before a glowing message scrawled itself out in looping green letters above my head.

Wise Woman's Hope

Yes! One of my choices! The third installment of a high fantasy trilogy we'd been waiting *ages* for.

Pizza after Town Hall? xo

The message disappeared with a scattering of green shimmers, and I pulled out my notepad.

Like you have to ask.
See you at the meeting. xx

Hamish returned and sank hard into the chair opposite mine. He huffed a breath and began unnecessarily retying his cravat. The telltale sign he was agitated.

"Why would Anon take those books? It doesn't make sense. You said Lacuna wanted them?"

"Eh, that's not exactly what she told me. He got them for her, but I don't think it was her idea. She's supposed to get a new tattoo soon and I think Anon thought the books would inspire her because she loves the Mortal Lands so much."

Hamish stopped fiddling with his wardrobe. "Why not just request access to the vault and take photos of some of the pages?"

"That's allowed?"

His head bobbed from side to side. "Frowned upon, but as long as a flash isn't used, it's acceptable."

"All I can think is that he did it because info about the Mortal Lands is blocked on search engines and Anon was just trying to help. The most peculiar part is that he had an accomplice. That *accomplice* is who I think got Anon mixed up in whatever resulted in him being attacked, and the one who might be connected to the murder."

Hamish reached for his cravat again, but I leaned over and stopped him. "You're sure it's connected?"

"No," I replied, sitting back in my chair, "but Sheriff Oliphant alluded to his suspicion that it might be. That's my other piece of info we need Mags for."

"Alright, if the accomplice used magic to change the titles or barcodes as it seems, I should be able to do a retracing spell and see if I can decipher how they managed it. That might give us some answers. Do you want to wait here?"

I looked behind him at a nest of computers. "Yeah, I'll wait. I want to check out the articles Kat has been writing lately on her blog. Do you know the web address?"

Hamish blinked at me. "You don't read her blog?"

"Not my cup of tea, I'm afraid. I like a classic, crisp newspaper."

Hamish frowned at me and stood. "It's saved in Favorites."

I walked over to the nearest computer and sat in the chair. "Favorites, Favorites..." I chanted, then made a popping sound with my lips. "Hamish!" I whisper-shouted. "What is *Favorites*?"

He was long gone. Alright. If Grandma can use a computer, so can I.

Blech. I even hated the texture of the mouse. Oh! But the clickity-clacks of the keyboard were nice as I typed 'Favorites' into the little white bar in the middle of the screen. All that got me was about twenty-seven books with 'favorites' in the title. Staring at the screen, I noticed a tiny pink heart up in the corner and clicked on it. This provided me with a list of long strings of letters and numbers— gobildy-goop all shoved together.

"Ah. *Websites.*" Can you tell I've used a computer a grand total of twice—during the week they became popular—and I have avoided them like the plague ever since? Yeah, me neither.

The fourth one down looked promising. It had *The Gloam Reporter* in the mishmash, anyway. I sent the cursor hovering over the blue jumble of words and clicked.

"Well, would ya' look at that?" These computers were actually pretty handy.

I won't be owning one anytime soon, though.

Kat had been busy. There were hundreds of articles on this website. Everything from town festivals and events to school happenings and even a few op-ed pieces that were pretty compelling.

I was still slogging through columns taking far too many notes when Hamish returned looking frazzled.

"B, it's about closing time. I've been working on the spell in between my duties but I haven't made much headway yet. You going to stick around longer or meet me at home later?"

I had no idea how to shut a computer down, so I just

stood up and pushed in my chair. "I have a couple of things to do. I'll meet you at home and we'll regroup with Mags before the town meeting."

"*Kitten tails.* I forgot about that. Is it about the murder?"

I shook my head and shouldered my bag. "Harvest Festival."

Hamish groaned. "That's worse."

I chuckled and left Hamish to his work—both librarian and Warlock.

A gust of wind blew into me as I left the library, sending my hair flying out around my head. By the time the gale died down, I was more than a little windswept, but just so pleased it wasn't hot out any longer. I rounded the corner to the square and saw more pumpkins had popped up, too.

Some pumpkins are placed around town by citizens, but most are simply a gift from our Autumn Goddess and we have no idea where they'll crop up or when. *Stonewood* was looking festive, too. A painter was decorating the window with a picturesque autumnal scene, and it looked like he'd hopped over there from the grocers because that window was done up as well.

Did I need more coffee before the trek back across the square? No, probably not. I wouldn't say no to a boba tea, though...

We weren't so fancy to have a designated boba shop in Gloam Hollow, but Tom's mom and leader of the Gloam Hollow Werewolf Pack owned the ice cream parlor and she makes a *mean* bubble tea.

I stopped in, pleased to find Linda Huang manning the counter herself.

"Blair!" She blew me a kiss. "Aren't you a sight for sore

eyes?" Then her face fell. "I am so sorry to hear you had to witness that grisly murder last night. Ice cream or boba?"

"Boba," I clarified, trying not to blanch at her seamless leap from murder to ice cream. "It doesn't make my top ten nights, I'll tell ya' that."

I glanced at the menu but already knew what I wanted: brown sugar boba. Apparently, Linda knew, too. She was already grabbing a cup with her adorable baby wolf logo.

"Hey, Linda," I started cautiously as she made my drink, "has Tom mentioned how Anon is doing? Or what's up between him and Maeve?" That last part was a major shot in the dark, but after last night's book club guest set-up by Linda's mother, Tina, I thought I'd give it a go.

Linda pursed her lips. "Maeve was in here this morning complaining that my *mother*"—she threw sufficient mocking into the word—"tried to set her and all of you book club girls up with a perfect stranger!"

"She sure did," I laughed. I didn't want to spill my friend's secrets any more than I already had, so I let Linda tell me what she knew.

"Mother must be angry with Tom, trying to aggravate him—you know how she is." Linda set my drink on the counter. "But I don't know what he did. And he won't answer my calls today, so I don't know how Anon is, either." I tried to hand her some moonstones but she waved me off. "On the house, sweetie. Sorry I couldn't be of more help."

CHAPTER 12

I was running out of time if I wanted to use the spell I'd found to follow the path behind the bakery up to the park.

Alas, I stopped at Misty Trees Road when I saw the street sign. If I took just the smallest of detours...

Before I could second-guess that tug on my Witchy instinct, I turned and headed on that detour, sipping my bubble tea.

About two houses down from Anon's, I ran into Sheriff Oliphant.

"Blair," he said, monotone, as he stopped on the sidewalk in front of me.

"Sheriff."

"Where ya' headed?"

"I don't have to answer that, legally speaking."

"Blair. I know you're headed to Anon's house." His gruff voice turned softer. "You need to keep out of this, darlin'."

"I'm not *in* anything."

"My tail you aren't. I already caught your mama here

twice today trying to take that boy muffins. I would think that's just the kind, neighborly thing to do if I didn't know better. But I do know better." He gave me the 'cop look.' "Stay out of this."

Alright, enough games. I tossed the last half of my boba in the trash bin behind Oliphant. "I just want to know how Anon is connected to the murder."

"That is—"

"I know you think he is," I challenged before he could fully respond.

After what felt like an eternity, Sheriff Oliphant shifted on his feet and looked down the narrow road to Anon's house. "I don't actually *know* anything yet. However, Anon might be squirrelly, but he's a Wendigo and he didn't even shift when attacked."

"Were there witnesses to confirm that? Wait, no. His shirt was intact, so he couldn't have shifted." I frowned. "His glasses weren't broken, either, even though he said he was tackled to the ground face first from behind. And no one took his wallet, so it wasn't a robbery."

I couldn't tell if Oliphant was impressed or dismayed. He probably didn't know which he was, either. "You've got a good eye, kid."

I mocked an exaggerated frown and he gently pushed my shoulder.

"I know you're not a kid anymore." Here came the giant, Sheriff Oliphant Sigh. "That boy in there is your friend. Now, I don't know if he's clammed up because he's genuinely traumatized, or because he's hiding something. But I've been here three times today and he won't say a word. If you can get him to talk to you, we'll have another conversation, you and I."

Yes! I cheered inwardly. *This is where Sheriff gives a little, and Blair takes a lot!* Thankfully, he knows this about me. And Wardwells in general. "You got it."

He groaned. "Please don't make me regret this."

"Never." And I trotted up to knock on Anon's door.

As I waited, I glanced over to see Sheriff Oliphant rounding the corner and headed for his cruiser parked down the way. Tom came to the door, but he only opened it a crack.

"Hey, B." He sounded...dazed? tired? "Anon isn't really feeling like any visitors right now."

"I'll only be a minute, promise." I gave him my best smile.

"Sorry. He's just feeling really down right now and asked me not to let anyone come over. I gotta respect that, you know?"

Could I take on a Werewolf? Tackle him to the ground and run in?

"Alright. Will you tell him I stopped by?"

"Sure thing."

"Thanks." Before he could shut the door in my face, I risked a sketchy question. "Is everything okay with you and Maeve?"

I swear the slit he was eyeing me through shrank. "Yep," he said too quickly. "Everything's great."

"It's just, she said—"

"I gotta go, B. I'll tell Anon you came by."

The door slammed and I stood there for a couple of minutes just staring at the wood grain. Blue. It was a nice shade of paint for a front door. Inviting.

Why were these two acting so *weird*?

I checked my watch and nearly yelped. I was due home

in less than an hour to debrief with Mags and Hamish in time for the town meeting.

Adjusting my messenger bag, I hurried off toward *The Copper Cauldron* and reminded myself to either leave my bag behind on my trek or take out some of the darn books making it so heavy.

Once I reached the square, I cut across the green past the gazebo, autumn leaves crunching beneath my wingtips. Thankfully, no one attempted to stop me and I made it to the apothecary in record time.

I threw my bag on the counter and gave Puck a quick peck on his head before flipping open my spellbook to the page I'd marked this morning.

Puck rolled over on the counter, yawning, and set to smacking the tassel on my bookmark. "Stop that," I said through a laugh. I ended up handing him the bookmark and relocating to the hearth.

With the book open on my lap, I carefully gathered all the ingredients I needed with my magic, gently plucking them from shelves. Once they were all aligned on the table in front of the fireplace, I rose and took my cauldron—yes, copper—and set it on its hook in the hearth.

The fire was already going, but only a little thing. I built it up the non-magical way—this works best for brewing—and began assembling my ingredients. One by one, I measured them out into the cauldron, careful to keep my intent firmly placed in my mind's eye.

The thing about magic is everyone has a spark of it. All one needs is a strong enough intent and the right spell. The problem lies in the fact that most people and creatures cannot seem to focus properly. It's a difficult thing to hold onto that wish, that vision, that purpose when worries, insecurity, hubris, or imagination set in. This results in very, very few magic-wielders outside of Witches and Warlocks. For some reason, we have less trouble in this department. Grandma Wardwell says it is the potency of our gift—it makes it easy to focus and makes things simple. But I like to think if we taught the rest of the mythical world how to hone in on what they want, they could have what we do.

That, however, is a forbidden thing to do in our world. Too many individuals would use it for ill intent—something each Witch and Warlock swears an oath not to do when they turn sixteen and have their Supernatural Baptism.

When the last ingredient was in the cauldron, I began stirring and chanting my spell, keeping my intent clear: *show me the path of what I seek.*

This, like all magic, has limitations. If it were as simple as using a location spell to find a perp, Sheriff Oliphant would have done so already. If you don't know who you're looking for, there really isn't any way to use a location spell. And if said person doesn't wish to be found, there are all manner of concealment spells.

Magic differs from person to person as well. I make potions for the most part. Sheriff Oliphant uses his innate well of magic and incantations. Hamish is a weaver—knitting together elements of magic for a desired effect. Etc, etc. It would take all day to explain the different ways Witches and Warlocks use their magic.

Since I had a hunch that the path from the park past the yellow house behind the bakery was used by our perp, I had a location I wanted to retrace. Without a person in mind, it was likely to reveal to me anyone who had taken that path in quite some time. It was not a perfect plan, but it was all I had at present.

With immense focus, I closed my eyes and began reciting my spell, every fiber of my being honed in on my intent. I could feel the magic course through me, pulling from my essence and flooding in from the ground beneath me, the air around me, and the ingredients in the cauldron. It felt warm, euphoric, like soaking in a hot bath after a long day. Ah, and the scent. Each spell has a scent unique to it. Most of the time, it's difficult to describe, and this occasion was no different. The best I could say is that it was almost like spiced oranges after bubbling in a simmer pot all day, then just a dash of wood smoke and dark chocolate.

Finally, the spell was complete and I opened my eyes.

No sooner had my voice drifted off into the rows of already-bottled elixirs, did a golden glow issue from the cauldron. The potion was ready. Using my favorite ladle—every Witch has one—I carefully poured a generous dosage into a vial and corked it. I didn't want to risk it spilling on my way to the alley.

There was no use wasting the rest of the potion, so I sent my magic to bottle and cork several more portions. Usually, I enjoy doing the next bit of the process by hand, but I was low on daylight, so I let my magic melt gooey globs of shimmering black wax to seal each cork. Then, *The Copper Cauldron* seal was pressed into the wax of each bottle. By the time I tucked the vial I planned to make use of into the pocket of my skirt, a lovely quill was writing the labels for me and lining the other bottles up on a shelf near the front.

Retracing Spell.

For my patrons, few as they were, the little bottles of potion would help them locate missing objects or pets by retracing the path they last recalled seeing their quarry. Things like that.

Headed for the back door of the shop, I paused, several thoughts colliding at once.

1 My shoes were impractical.

2 I should lock the front door.

3 What was my excuse if someone intercepted me?

All easy enough to handle. I took off my wingtips and summoned a pair of combat-style boots. "Hmm." Though mixing feminine and masculine pieces creates a lovely ensemble, this wasn't working for me. Alas, it was not my biggest concern.

Shoes—check.

I spelled the front door of *The Cauldron* locked. Check.

Excuse? Out for a stroll could work, but next to someone's house? Let's just hope I wasn't seen during that part of the excursion. We'll count that as checked too.

"Be good," I told Puck as I strode to the back.

I am but a beast you cannot dream to tame, he purred.

I snorted. "Says the cat taking a nap and quoting poetry."

Out in the alley that doubled as a street, I had a choice to make. I could go back through the shop and invoke the power of the potion where the body was found in the hope it would show me which way the murderer went, or I could begin in the park as originally planned, in the hope it would show me Anon's attacker fleeing from the park in this direction.

In the end, I had to choose the park. The murder happened in front of *Toil & Truffle*, not behind it. My hunch was weak at best, but it couldn't be a coincidence that the park Anon was attacked in had a convenient little trail that let out into this alley behind the square where an as-yet-unidentified body showed up soon after. I was determined to make sense of it.

Without using the potion yet, I followed the path of my suspicions. Passing the yellow house and trying to look as inconspicuous as possible, I ducked down the narrow path at the house's side, walking as quietly as I could over the brush and crunching leaves.

My heart was hammering against my ribs, but I tried to traverse slowly—looking for anything in the natural that could be out of place. I couldn't make out any distinct trail in the dirt, but the leaves had been falling in droves since yesterday. Any trodden path would likely be covered up by now.

It wasn't long before the path spilled out into the treeline of the park. The sun was considering its slumbering decline, but kids were still running through the grass. A few families picnicked, enjoying the retreat of summer. There were even a couple of readers on the cluster of benches where the paramedic had helped Anon last night.

One of them happened to be Maeve.

"*Bingpot*," I whispered to myself. (Another Grandma Wardwell word, but this time less a curse and more a celebration.)

Invoking a spell to find a murderer with so many others around was ill-advised, but no one would think anything of me sitting with my Vampire friend to discuss a book.

I strolled over, trying to look nonchalant, but as soon as I approached Maeve, she frowned at me with narrowed eyes. "What are you up to?"

"Lovely to see you too, *friend*."

"Let me rephrase, then. Why do you look so dubious?"

Now, I love Maeve like a sister, and I might come off as a

meddlesome kind of Witch, but I do actually prefer to keep my own doings quite private. It's not that I didn't trust Maeve to keep what I was doing a secret, but her Werewolf boyfriend was high on my list of suspicious happenings as of the last couple of days. In the crime novels I like to read, the detective is always mum on the details, keeping the specific somethings extra close to his (or her!) chest.

I sat down on the opposite side of the bench. "Just go back to your reading." I glanced at the title, it was the book club pick, *Wise Woman's Hope*. "Are you enjoying it, by the way?" (C'mon, how could I pass up any opportunity to talk books?)

Maeve flipped it over to look at the cover then flipped it back. "Undecided. I think I rather like the morally gray guy in this one, but I think I'm supposed to be falling for the white knight character."

Call me dramatic. Call me a Witch with an over-active imagination, but was her statement some sort of dark omen? I shivered. "I can't wait to get started on it."

I pulled the potion out of my pocket and dumped some in my hands as if it were lotion. Gently but thoroughly, I rubbed it into my skin, my hands turning a distinct neon green as my magic silently called on the spell. Thankfully, I'd had the forethought to add a concealment component to the magic, so it would only reveal a trail (of neon green) to the invoker of the potion—because Maeve was watching me *very* carefully.

When I stood up and tried to tell Maeve I'd see her at the town meeting later, she screwed up her face like she'd eaten a lemon. "You walked into the park to sit on a bench and put on lotion and then leave?"

Yikes, I needed to get better at this sleuthing stuff. "No,"

I said with a bit too much force. "I went on a walk to clear my head and saw my *friend* at the park, so I stopped over. But I'm going to be late meeting Hamish and Maggie, so I need to go already."

Well, that lie came too easily. Maybe I'm not quite so bad at this? A little knot of guilt curled up next to the lingering dread in my gut. I started to say I was sorry for being so harsh with my tone but then remembered my deal with Aramis. *You have just as much right to exist and speak your mind as anyone else*, he'd said. Maeve had spoken her mind, and I'd spoken mine. I would not apologize when it was unnecessary.

"Okay," Maeve finally said with a hint of attitude. "See ya'."

You know what, I did not have time for pettiness. My neon green magic was leaking from my hands and making an interesting set of trails, swipes, and strokes all over the park and into the treeline.

CHAPTER 13

A smattering of trails littered the park.

One for every person that had entered since the night of the attack, and the number was many. Not only had a small crowd gathered last night after it happened but the sheriff and paramedic had come, too. Then, all those who had come throughout the day today in celebration of cooler weather. Since the intent while brewing my potion had a distinct connection to Anon and the murder, those trails were, thank Goddess, brighter—more distinct.

With Maeve's intense attention still pinned on me, I couldn't thoroughly investigate the magic in the park, but I took a quick mental note of the swirling mess of green. There was no doubt it had to be where Anon was attacked. From what I could gather in just a couple of glances, the short, stark smudges were Anon's movements, and the other, more swooping trail was his attacker. There was, however, a very distinct separation—two trails leading away from Anon's, which stopped abruptly, becoming a big blob. Only a light dusting led from it to the bench he'd been seated on when I saw him.

I couldn't spend any more time looking at it without appearing suspicious. Both trails aside from Anon's blob led in the direction I expected them to—back toward the treeline. I followed them with quick steps into the patch of woods that acted as a barrier between the park and the row of homes bordering the alley.

A few paces into the woods, right before the narrow pathway I'd followed from the back of the bakery to the park, one of the trails completely stopped. Vanished. It was puzzling, but I didn't stop for long. Before the magic could fade, I rushed to follow the other green trail down the leaf-littered path, past the side of the quaint yellow house. It darted across the alley, and I followed it past the bakery's back door, past Art's, and past my shop's back entrance, all the way to the back of the café, where it, like the other trail, vanished.

I could feel my pulse in my fingers, in my temples. A bit short of breath from my quick pace, I stopped, thinking hard. It didn't lead all the way to the back door of the café, just right up to where I was now standing. Had there been a vehicle of some kind back here? It was a narrow lane and it would be a tight squeeze, but it was possible.

Most Gloam Hollow residents never used vehicles aside from bicycles or perhaps a moped or motorcycle. Deliveries were rare aside from those at the grocer, and most shop owners made their goods by hand. It would make sense if a café needed more deliveries, though. Surely Aramis didn't make his own ketchup packets and silverware. I'd never seen construction supplies dropped off in the square, so at least lumber and things had to have been delivered back here. There were other faint paths of footsteps, but not many, and most were so transparent they must have been older. Except for a set of two that were darker, yet still not nearly as obvious as the one that had disappeared. Those led from where I stood on the narrow road, up to the door.

"The oven!" Aramis had an oven delivery this morning. Was it connected? Had the perp fled in a truck, or hidden in one all night and fled this morning after the oven delivery?

None of this confirmed any real connection to the murder, either. It happened in *front* of *Toil & Truffle*.

Frustrated, I growled and blew out a breath.

While the magic still held, I rushed to the back door of the apothecary and spelled it open. I ran through, calling a half-hearted greeting to Puck—and Albis, who'd apparently joined him—launching myself out the front door. Old Mrs. Comfrey gave a startled '*oh dear*' when I almost bowled into her. With a mumbled apology, I kept my eyes glued on a perfect path from the blob of green so dark it was almost black in front of the bakery, all the way to Art's candy shop, where it disappeared under the door.

Art? *Art*? No way. There was zero chance frail Art, our wizened and wobbly Elf had murdered a man probably half his age or younger.

Sure, we leave our front doors unlocked during the day most of the time, even if we're not there, but not at close to ten o'clock. And though many mystical creatures have powers of various kinds, all the locks in this town have been spelled by a Wardwell or a Tuttle to be in single command of their owner and those their owner allows. Getting in without express permission would be nearly impossible.

I wondered vaguely who had spelled Aramis's locks when he came to town.

I made a beeline for Art's, stepping through the fading magic, but the CLOSED sign was already out. He must have closed up early to grab some dinner and head to the town meeting.

"*Son of a monkey*," I muttered.

The trail in the alley hadn't led all the way to Art's, though. Frustration grabbed me by the knot of dread in my stomach and squeezed.

I made my way back through the apothecary and over to where the trail abruptly stopped coming from the park. Maybe they just weren't connected. A peculiar coincidence.

Walking in a slow, zig-zag, I scanned the ground and even the air for signs of magic or...*anything*. That's when I saw, hardly noticeable at all, three drops on the ground.

Rust-colored stains.

Aramis

"Henry, if you don't get out of my office right this second, I swear I'm going to turn you to stone."

"You wouldn't dare," the pesky ghost said, examining his nails as he sat on my desk. "It wouldn't work, anyway. I'm dead." The sass in his last word had me gritting my teeth.

I growled at him, "Test me, then." When I reached one hand up to touch the wrap covering my dreads that could *so easily* shift into deadly vipers, the ghost vanished with a little *pop*, like a soap bubble. Smug, I returned to my ledger, immensely glad Steven couldn't see Henry.

Goddess, the trouble I'd have if those two could gab together.

Blair hadn't told me how old Henry had died, and he claimed he couldn't recall, but I was determined to find out. Maybe I could help him find everlasting peace before opening night so he'd *go away*.

I could at least gather that he died somewhere in the distant past considering his vintage clothing. Although judging by this town, he could have just been in costume when he perished.

Knuckles rapped on the doorjamb to my office. Kenny, my head of construction. A six-and-a-half foot tall Orc, walking around in the skin of a city biker. Just about every inch of Kenny is covered in tattoos and I would guess this town is going to be glad when he leaves. Little do they know he has the softest heart of anyone I've ever met—unless you mess with someone he cares about. I once caught him crying during a movie about baby ducks, but I'd also seen Kenny do some difficult things to protect others as well.

"What can I do ya' for, Kenny?"

"We're headed out, Dread. Everything is in tip-top shape and that old fart of a mayor says you pass inspection."

"That's excellent news." I stood and rounded the desk. "I'm sorry to see you go, though. It's been nice having you around again." I reached out my hand and Kenny took it, pulling me in to clap me hard on the back.

"Be good, Dread. Know I've always got your back and the second I leave here, your location is gone from memory, you hear?"

"I hear you." I squeezed his shoulder and we parted.

His voice lowered to a menacing whisper. "But if you need me, I'll be back and ready to knock heads."

"I've got you on speed dial, Ken."

"Alright. We're out then, Brother. Don't let that small fry

sheriff push your buttons, either." His face contorted. "And uh, just so you know...that mayor won't leave 'till he speaks with you."

I groaned. "I'll walk you out, then."

Mayor Bill Winslow sat at my counter looking like he'd rather have his fingernails pulled off than be in my café. Kenny and the other construction guys grabbed the last of their tools and left out the back.

"Good riddance," Winslow muttered to their backs.

"Can I help you, Winslow?" I asked shortly.

The round, grumpy man stood from his stool and thrust a bright orange paper into my hands. "I'm afraid we have some things to discuss."

$\sim$

Blair

"Is the sheriff here?" I asked breathlessly without greeting Mrs. Cobblepot.

"Hello, dear," she said, smiling up at me from behind her computer. "I'm afraid not. He had a few things to look into before going to Town Hall for the meeting."

I was due to meet Hamish and Maggie in fifteen minutes. What I'd found would have to wait.

"Okay. Could you have him come by *Moonrise Manor* after the meeting?" Surely Mom wouldn't mind Corbin crashing our pizza night for a minute.

"Of course, dear. I'll just send him a message."

Mrs. Cobblepot pulled out a cell phone that looked huge in her hands. Her fingers deftly slid across the screen and I marveled at her aptitude for technology. That message would have taken me five minutes to type out, but she set her phone down in just a few seconds and smiled up at me. She didn't even have a chance to speak before it dinged.

"He says that will be fine."

I bid Mrs. Cobblepot farewell and headed for home.

Maggie was in the workshop when I arrived, murmuring to one of her plant babes. Like her mother, Mags had an affinity for growing things, yet she harbored a deep hatred for being out *in* nature. Her poultices were coveted almost as much as Aunt Millie's florals, and I used several of her recipes to stock the apothecary. Her knack for the natural also made Mags a stylist who could make hair of any kind do just about anything she wanted it to. After she'd worked at Gloam Hollow's premier salon for a while and gained some notoriety, we all expected her to open her own posh studio. But Mags was happy where she was. She could use her gifts without being outdoors and still had time to tinker with potions and poultices.

"Hey, B. Let me take Rachelle here"—she held up a pot with glowing red flowers—"to the greenhouse for some warmth and I'll meet you in the kitchen. I think Hamish is in the library."

Shocker there. I picked up a marble mortar and pestle and peered inside. The crushed herbs at the bottom didn't look familiar, so I sniffed the paste. Though it was vaguely similar to basil, the scent also carried an undercurrent not unlike the fetid odor of comfrey.

"Grandma was here earlier," Maggie said as she cradled her plant in the doorway leading to the garden. "She's trying to see if she can alter spells using some of Mom's cross-bred herbs."

"It smells dreadful," I said, setting the mortar down with my nose wrinkled.

Maggie laughed. "It does indeed."

I climbed the stairs up to the library and found Hamish up in the tree. Aunt Millie had planted a tree in the middle of Wardwell Cottage when we were children, and Grandma directed the roots where to go. This spell took some maintenance from one or more of us at times so the roots didn't obstruct our living spaces, but for the most part, the trunk jutted from the corner of the workshop up to the second floor, its branches unfurling up in the library.

"We're going to have to cut a hole to the third floor soon," I told Hamish.

He looked over his book at me. "Chester will be livid."

The third floor was his domain, but a lonely ghost cat might just like tree branches to climb.

"Are you ready for our debrief?"

Hamish snorted and shook his head at me. "You sound like a proper detective, Cousin." He levitated down from the tree and we made our way to the kitchen to wait for Mags.

"How do you think the town meeting will go tonight?" I asked as I pulled down a jar of coffee beans and a jar of tea leaves from the cabinet.

Hamish filled a kettle with water and set it on the stove to boil. "About like they always do. Mayhem and madness."

The kettle sang a few minutes later and I poured steaming water over the leaves Hamish had put in his favorite steeper—a dapper-looking penguin. Maggie came in, cheery as could be, and sat next to Hamish at the table while I scooped coffee grounds out of the grinder and put them in a brown paper filter.

"How was your day, hm?" I asked neither of them in particular as I set to pouring the water over the grounds.

"The salon was swamped," Maggie groaned. "I was lucky Stacey wanted to close for the meeting tonight or I never would have gotten out of there."

"Best client?" Hamish asked, taking a sip of his tea.

This was a game we played often. 'Best client' did not, in fact, mean best. It meant the one with the most outlandish story, the worst possible behavior, or—and this was usually it—the one with the best town gossip.

I poured coffee into a mustard mug with little bees on it —Maggie's favorite—as I listened to her talk. "Easy!" She waved her hands around wildly as she spoke. "Mrs. Stalbach is convinced the murderer is the one who put George Carter's flamingo on the sheriff's roof." Hamish and I both laughed and I slid the mug to her. "She had this outlandish idea that the victim is the one who sold George the flamingo since *apparently* he got it on vacation on the coast somewhere."

"So the flamingo salesman clearly had a vendetta," I put in jokingly, sitting down with my own mug of coffee. (A little cauldron with a handle and lid, if you're wondering. Lots of whipped cream, too.)

Maggie snapped and pointed at me. "Detective Blair on the case."

"Sor–" I caught myself before I could apologize. Instead, I asked myself inwardly if I'd done anything worth apologizing for. Then I sat up straighter because *no*, I had not. "Hamish," I said instead, "speaking of detective work... Did you figure out the spell used on the library books?"

"What spell?" Maggie asked, eyes wide with intrigue.

We caught her up on the happenings with Anon and the Mortal Lands books.

Hamish shook his head, tapping his teacup with an idle finger. "All I could figure out is that the person used a complicated shifting spell to flip-flop the titles and barcodes of the books. In doing so, Anon actually did check out the books listed, as the metadata matches the barcodes on those books." He huffed a laugh. "It's clever really."

"Is that something Anon is capable of?" Maggie asked, looking between us. "He's a Wendigo."

"No," I clarified, stirring my coffee with a little gold spoon. "According to Lacuna, he had an accomplice."

"So, Witch or Warlock, then?"

Hamish shrugged. "Maybe. There was a hefty cloaking spell mixed in. One I didn't recognize the properties or signature of."

In a way, most magic has a signature of sorts that points to the certain being that cast it. This isn't an exact science and doesn't work if it's a person using someone else's potion, but, once you get to know someone's magic—see it often enough—you can sense little defining things within it. Aunt Millie's magic always has earth tones and an almost imperceptible scent of soil. Maggie's almost always has an iridescence to it, like gossamer wings. Things like that.

"What did the unfamiliar signature look like?" I asked, curling my legs up against my chest as I reclined in my chair.

"It..." Hamish trailed off, his face twisted up in thought. "It was wiggly. Like a bunch of snakes."

My stomach dropped to my toes.

"Do you think it was a creature with magic that isn't a

Witch or Warlock?" Maggie asked, and I was grateful because my mouth was suddenly filled with cotton.

"It definitely didn't seem like Witch magic. Certainly not Tuttle or Wardwell."

There were a few other Witch families in town, but their magic wasn't nearly as strong.

I sipped my coffee trying to clear my clogged throat, one loud thought screaming in my head like a banshee: *Do Dread Monsters have magic?*

"What did you find out from Kat?" Hamish changed the subject.

"Ugh." Mags pushed the hair out of her eyes. "Nothing. No one really knows a thing, not even who the guy is. Kat asked around relentlessly all day, but Sheriff threatened to throw her in that sorry excuse for a holding cell if she didn't stop pestering people."

"I might know a little about the guy," I said, wincing because they both turned on me like I was the killer myself.

"The victim?" Maggie screeched.

"And you've just kept it to yourself all day?" Hamish sniped.

"Woah now, ponies." I held up a hand to halt their attack. "Sheriff Oliphant gave me a little information. He told me not to share it with anyone, but obviously, I'm not going to listen to that when it comes to you two."

"You *better* tell us," Maggie snipped.

"It does not leave this family though, do you understand?" I still didn't want Kat involved. The more I thought about including her, even at a distance this morning, the more I regretted it. "And leave Kat out of everything going forward. Okay?"

Hamish and Maggie looked at each other strangely before nodding.

I broke down what Sheriff Oliphant told me about the victim being from out of town and a John Doe right now. I told them about his warning not to speak about it with anyone, most of all Anon.

"That's so suspicious," Maggie said in a hushed tone.

"It has to be connected then, right?"

I nodded at Anon. "I have even more evidence to support that theory…"

The next half hour was spent rehashing every tiny moment of my day with my cousins. Except the little detail of where I found the spots of blood. I only told them it was in the alleyway and not behind the café. I was still debating telling Sheriff Oliphant that part, too. Or about the blood at all. It made Aramis look extremely guilty. But it wasn't my job to protect him, especially if he *was* guilty.

When I'd finished the description of the victim, Maggie and Hamish both agreed they hadn't seen anyone like that around town. I knew they wouldn't, not without that distinctive tattoo on his wrist that I was also keeping to myself. My Witch's intuition wouldn't let up on that point.

"Do you know his race?" Hamish asked.

"No, but surely Sheriff does by now. I asked him to meet me at the inn after the town meeting."

"Speaking of…" Maggie stood. "We better get going."

"Wait!" I dropped my feet to the floor and stood. "I need to change clothes."

"Um, why?" Mags asked, eyeing my outfit.

"Because every outing is a new opportunity to wear a different outfit, of course."

G loam Hollow Town Hall is an old tavern.

Yep. A medieval stone building complete with an abandoned watermill, brew kettle, and a perky seagull weathervane. Are we anywhere near the sea? Nope. Is the tavern older than Gloam Hollow? Probably.

According to Hamish, sometime long ago the coast came all the way up to where The Hollow is now. There are a few other buildings about as old as the tavern—er, Town Hall—and they have similar nautical elements that back up Hamish's claims. Most likely, we learned about all of this in school, but I only heard about half of what was said in boring classes, as I usually had an open fiction book hidden under my desk.

Grandma also backs up Hamish's claim, and her theory is that the dragon on Draak Summit selected the mountains for her treasure, but frowned upon such a large amount of water nearby. She claims the dragon essentially evaporated the water with her fire breath until that drove the edge of the sea back, leaving only a lake behind.

In Grandma's defense, the lake *is* salt water, and the sea is a reasonable enough distance away to add credibility to her story.

"Girl, you look like a million moonstones!" Katarina squealed at me as we joined the flow of people filing into Town Hall.

I'd kept the black tights but switched out my plaid skirt for a short overall romper of maroon velvet, paired with a black turtleneck underneath and a mustard cardigan over. My combat boots had been switched out for a pair of Witchy black ankle boots stitched with a crescent moon. I even had on my seldom-worn witch hat, lilting floppily and perfectly to the side. When you dress for yourself, what you wear always adds a spell of elation to any event—especially the mundane ones.

Adjusting my glasses, I muttered, "Thanks, Kat." Personally, I was quite fond of my wardrobe change, but I had the distinct feeling that Katarina was only buttering me up. For what, I couldn't guess.

"Soooo." She knocked her shoulder into mine playfully as we found seats in the crowded hall. "Heard you were acting strangely in the park this afternoon and that you stopped by the sheriff's office soon after."

She was smiling, but I suddenly felt a deep urge to punch her in her pretty white teeth. "Being a busybody is not the same as gathering the news, Katarina," I snapped. I immediately considered apologizing but, lo and behold, I caught sight of Aramis across the room and I did no such thing. Though, I might actually constitute this occasion as one where I *should* have apologized. "If you'll excuse me," I said instead and walked away.

Aramis lifted his hand in what I'd call a 'too cool to

wave' wave as one corner of his mouth dragged upward a little. I reminded myself fourteen times as I headed in his direction and he in mine that he could be a murderer. He met me halfway across the cavernous beam-and-stone hall that used to sell ale and mead.

"At a town meeting, huh?" I said cheekily. "I guess you're official then."

Aramis held up a bright orange piece of paper. "I'm here because that goon Winslow came into the café today to inform me I can't put my sign up until after this Harvest Festival."

I gave him my best mock-sympathy frown. "Ooo, yeah. Everyone puts up decorations for the festival. Each business essentially becomes a carnival stand."

The Dread Monster's green eyes went wide. I'd never seen his face be so expressive. "*What*? No, no, no." His loosely wrapped hair swayed with the movement of his head and I wondered if he was in danger of shifting. "I'm set to open in a couple of weeks, I can't do all that."

With a little shrug, I started to say I'd help him but thought better of it. "Usually, the Tuttles, Wardwells, and anyone else with magic in town help out. It makes quick work of setting up and tearing down."

Aramis blew out a breath, dropping his arm until the orange notice in his hand slapped against his leg. "Do I need to postpone opening? This is crazy."

"Attention! Attention, everyone! Find your seats!"

Oh, good. Grandma is the mediator tonight. She will put a swift stop to any unnecessary mayhem. Well, that, or be the cause of it. Fifty-fifty chance there.

Everyone was shuffling around and the remaining few seats filled up quickly. There were two left in the middle of a row, so I grabbed the long sleeve of Aramis's shirt without thinking and tugged him toward them. We tripped over feet and knocked knees with several people before landing in the empty, creaky chairs.

Grandma Wardwell, a spry little thing with wild white hair just like Maggie's silvery locks, stood on the platform behind a podium and banged her gavel. "Gloam Hollow Town Meeting Number 18,362 is officially in session. As always, we will handle matters on the agenda first." She pointed to the whiteboard next to her that read:

- Goose-Toad Hybrids
- Harvest Festival
- New Guy

Aramis elbowed me. "Tell me that's not me they have on that board." His eyes were wide and full of an appropriate level of fear.

I grimaced. "Maybe not?" Yeah, right.

"Then," Grandma went on, "we will open the floor for issues and matters to be presented. Before we begin, Sheriff Oliphant has one order of business to address."

Grandma moved back from the podium and the sheriff stepped up. "Good evening." He leaned too close to the microphone and the feedback made everyone wince. "Sorry folks. I'll be quick. I know our beloved Hollow saw some scary things yesterday and I would like to take this opportunity to tell you that there is no reason to be frightened. We have matters under control."

Did we? I risked a glance at Aramis and I'd swear I saw him fidget.

"I know it's been the talk of the town all day, but we will not be discussing the events of last night in this meeting. Is that clear?"

Murmurs echoed throughout the room and I looked around to find Mom sitting with Aunt Moira and Hamish. Mags was behind them, sandwiched between Maeve and Katarina. I didn't see Aunt Millie, she was probably still on the hiking trails. Lacuna was absent, too, but she hardly ever came to town meetings, choosing instead to keep *Stonewood* open so everyone had a place to go and cross-examine the meeting agenda afterward. As expected, Anon and Tom were nowhere to be seen, either.

Evidently satisfied he had as much agreement as he was liable to get, Sheriff Oliphant gave the floor back to Grandma.

"First order of business: Goose-Toad Hybrids," she said simply as if it wasn't the most absurd thing listed on the whiteboard. I guess for Gloam Hollow, it really wasn't that bananas.

Mayor Bill Winslow waddled up to the podium. "Thank you, Penelope. There have been a multitude of complaints regarding the goose-toad hybrids that have invaded Ramsett Creek. We have not yet discovered how they got there, but we are getting to the bottom of it. Until then, we advise everyone to steer clear of the area, especially if you have small children. If the problem is not resolved within a fortnight, we will take Werewolf and Vampire volunteers to eradicate the issue."

Aramis looked at me, his brows high. "Gruesome."

Judging by the similar disgusted looks around the hall, many were thinking the same. I looked back at Maeve to find her fangs extended. Luke, a few rows ahead of her, looked as if he might shift into his Were' form at any moment.

Bill stepped back and Grandma came forward again.

"Any comments on the hybrids in Ramsett Creek?" There were a couple of coughs and a baby Troll let out a babble toward the back, but no one came forward. "Alright. Second order of business: The Harvest Festival. Mr. Mayor?"

Bill came up again and adjusted the mic, sending another screech through the speakers. Aramis tugged at his ear. "Ladies and gentlemen, as you well know, the Harvest Festival is our biggest festival of the year. It draws in many tourists and brings joy to our community. As usual, participation is mandatory and each shop and home *will be decorated.*"

He put so much emphasis on the last three words that he might as well have banged the gavel for each one. Aramis squirmed in his seat and groaned.

"Pumpkins are already popping up in droves, so we need to get on it. We all know the weather could shift to winter or back to summer for all we know at any time, so we have one week to get all decorations up, and the festival will begin next Starday and go the entire week."

"Oh, come *on*," Aramis fumed harshly, almost launching out of his seat. He looked at me as several people around us shot him dirty looks. "That's the week I'm supposed to open. He knows that!"

"As I was *saying*," Bill groused, apparently witnessing Aramis's minor outburst, "participation is mandatory and we need everyone working overtime to ensure word gets out to the surrounding area and this festival works like a well-oiled machine. I will not have a disaster similar to four years ago."

"Do I even want to know?" Aramis whispered as Bill droned on about his lofty expectations.

"Not unless you'd like him to talk for six hours straight

about how the hotdogs were spoiled and the entire town was sick for a week, and the tourists got snowed in because winter showed up in the middle of the festival. The tourists had to sleep in the shops while green in the face for days."

"Brutal..."

"You have no idea. There's an Orc puke stain under one of my rugs in the apothecary that even magic couldn't get out."

"That might be worse than the geese-toad genocide."

I laughed, clapping a hand over my mouth to stifle it.

"Are you two quite finished?" Bill griped at us from the podium. Every. Single.Person turned to look at us. How much trouble would I be in if I disappeared on the spot?

"Go on, Winslow," Aramis drawled lazily.

I heard several whispers around us offering mixed views of '*the new guy.*'

"Sign-up sheets will be posted in the back at the end of the meeting to claim your theme and activity. If you have not signed up by the end of the week, you will be assigned one." Bill glared at Aramis. "And that brings us to our last item on the agenda." He looked to Grandma, who gave him one of those *mother* looks.

"You're right there," I heard her say with a plethora of Wardwell Sass before she got to the mic. "You could have just said it yourself." She sighed, the mic crackling. "Last order of business:"—another exasperated glare at Bill—"The New Guy." She and Bill switched places yet again.

"This should be fun," Aramis muttered sarcastically, but he looked almost amused as if maybe he would get a smidgen of joy out of the impending clash.

"I would like to motion that Aramis Hawthorne postpone the opening of his as-yet-unnamed café—"

He was cut off when Aramis stood. "It's not unnamed, Winslow. You saw the sign yourself not four hours ago. *The Spectre Café*."

"Ah." Bill smiled in an oily sort of way and my stomach dropped. "Isn't that fitting, then?" I saw the realization on Aramis's face just before Bill went on. He'd been *had*. "I move that Mr. Hawthorne postpones the opening of *The Spectre Café*, instead using the spot as a Harvest Festival haunted house, the ghost of Henry Wigglesworth as his star."

Yup. Aramis walked right into that one.

"Are you discriminating because I'm the new guy? This is nuts! I can easily just put up a few scarecrows or hay bales or something, I don't have to delay my opening."

Bill completely and thoroughly ignored him. "All in favor of a haunted café at *The Spectre*?"

A resounding 'aye' shot across the room. Aramis turned in a slow half-circle, stunned.

The gavel banged. "Motion passes!"

And Aramis dropped into his chair. He looked too flabbergasted to be angry.

I patted his shoulder. "There, there."

He was staring slack-jawed at his clasped fists when Grandma bustled back to the podium.

"We will now open the floor to the public. If you have a concern, please stand."

I honestly expected Aramis to pop up out of his seat, but he was still perplexed, like he didn't even know what just happened to him. I felt bad for the guy. I could get the apothecary and even the cottage decorated in a jiff. Then I could help Aramis.

Provided he wasn't the murderer... *Spaghetti squash,* I had to stop forgetting he was a suspect!

Sweet Art stood from his seat, a little worse for the wear.

"Arty," Grandma said, "you have the floor, dear."

Kendall, Katarina's Faerie sister, hopped up from the front row and took a microphone over to Art. In truth, the microphones were entirely unnecessary, but we liked to pretend we were big-city sometimes, I suppose.

After a few hacking coughs, Art spoke—and not into the microphone. He forgot he was holding it and just talked normally. "Somebody unlocked my candy shop last night!"

Confused murmurs went through the room. I looked over my shoulder and locked eyes with Hamish. He mouthed *how?* and I quickly swung around to look at Sheriff Oliphant, who was paying very close attention.

"Now, Arty," Grandma said placatingly, "that building was spelled by a Witch ages ago to only open by your permission. Are you sure you didn't just leave it unlocked?"

"Yes, Pen, I am certain I did not leave it unlocked. It was spelled by the Wardwells or Tuttles and you know it, so it had to be one of you!"

Gasps went through the room. Ms. Lilly Tuttle stood so quickly that her husband had to steady her chair. "Don't you throw accusations around unless you can back them up, old man!"

"Lillian!" Mom stood from her seat, Moira and Hamish following suit.

"Guess it's my turn in the hubbub," I said out the side of my mouth to Aramis and stood, too. Mags followed, then Lilly's daughter, Betty Tuttle, and Grandma Tuttle—albeit that one took some time getting out of her chair.

Immediately, it was Tuttle versus Wardwell and Witches

versus Art. Nobody knew which family had spelled the place and the entire thing was getting out of hand.

"It's always the same with you Wardwells," Grandma Tuttle croaked, then spat at her feet in dismissal, but half of the glob landed in the puffy hair of the woman in front of her.

"You Tuttles cast shoddy spells, anyway!" Moira was shouting at Lilly, Mom trying to hold her back. "Get off me, Minerva! Lilly needs another new nose and I'm happy to oblige!"

"You Wardwells are the ones with slippery magic! Can't even keep a man!" Lilly shot back. Hamish launched over a row of chairs and I startled forward, sending a rope of magic out to lasso him before he could throttle Ms. Lilly.

I did, however, manage to keep my trap shut. I suspected what happened at Art's was far worse than which one of our families cast the spell on his locks. I also knew Mom, Moira, and Lilly would all be the best of friends again in a day or two.

"Everyone just calm down!" Grandma ordered, banging her gavel.

About eight or nine bangs in, Sheriff Oliphant came over the mic, his voice booming. "Enough! That's it. Time to go home, everyone!"

"Meeting adjourned!" Grandma shouted over the din, banging the gavel one more time.

"But my shop!" Art was complaining. Sheriff Oliphant headed toward him while Aramis and I made our way to the door.

CHAPTER 15

The crowd in front of the sign-up sheets for Harvest Festival themes was synonymous with the Wall of Death at a hardcore concert.

"Shove over, Oscar," Lawrence Mosgrove—a Griffin—was shouting, throwing elbows.

"Why should you get to have the snowglobe theme, Lawrence? *I'm* the Yeti!"

Aramis had stopped to gawk at the melee blocking our way out of Town Hall. He turned to me with one brow raised. "At least I don't have to sign up for a theme, I guess."

"Silver lining," I chirped in agreement, weaving my way through the throng, him close at my heels.

When we finally made it outdoors, I realized how stuffy it had been in the hall, all those creatures crowded in. We usually head to *Stonewood* to scrutinize town meetings afterward, but I had a pizza date with Mom and a different sort of meeting with Sheriff Oliphant on my agenda.

Had it really only been a day since the murder? It felt like forty years. I rubbed at my tired eyes behind my glasses, only realizing afterward that I'd probably smudged my mascara.

"Same," Aramis said, gesturing to my sleepy eyes as Maggie and Hamish walked up.

I could tell Hamish was ticked that I'd roped him like cattle, but he was proper enough not to mention it in front of the new guy in town. (And yet, he *wasn't* proper enough not to launch himself over chairs at a Witch twice his age.)

"Hey guys, this is Aramis Hawthorne," I said.

"Yeah, we gathered that," Mags giggled and held out her hand. "Margaret Wardwell, but you can call me Maggie."

Aramis shook her hand, then turned to hold his out to Hamish.

"Hamish Wardwell." His voice was so serious I almost laughed.

"That would make you all...siblings?" Aramis asked, but I could tell he was confused by how different I looked from my cousins.

"Cousins," Maggie answered. "Our mothers are sisters."

"Yeah, the crazy Witches in a tussle not five minutes ago," I snorted.

Aramis made that face that we all make when we realize we've forgotten something simple. "Ah, that's right. Witches and Warlocks are matriarchal."

Correct. Most familial lines take the last names of the fathers, but Witch magic all comes from women, so even the Warlocks take their mother's last name. Most Warlocks and other creatures that marry a Witch take their last name as well. I *love* that about our mystical race.

Aramis stifled a yawn. "It's nice to meet you two." He turned to me. "I have to go regroup or get a lobotomy after that debacle."

I laughed, and so did Maggie and Hamish. "Understandable. Word of advice, don't tell Henry about the haunted café until you've had some sleep and a *lot* of coffee."

Aramis groaned. "The worst part is he figured out I live in the apartment above the café. He sits on the stairs and waits for me every morning."

"Sounds about right," Hamish chuckled.

"Alright. I'll see you guys later," he said to Hamish and Maggie, then to me, "We're still on for Starday?"

I could feel my cousins' eyes slowly widening. "Um, yep. Yes. Seven o'clock, right?"

"Perfect. Goodnight, guys." Aramis looked both ways—as if there might actually be traffic in Gloam Hollow—and crossed the street with his hands in his pockets.

As soon as he was out of earshot, Maggie gripped my arm, standing an inch from my face. "Care to share with the class?"

"Yeah… I forgot to mention he invited me and a couple of 'plus ones' to taste-test his menu this weekend. He wants to do a sort of soft launch before the big opening."

"Obviously, you've chosen us, right?" Hamish tugged at my other arm and I shook them both off.

"Obviously." I checked my watch. "I have to go meet Mom at the inn, I'll see you guys at home?"

"Yeah," Maggie said, already headed back into Town Hall. "Now that the crowd has thinned, I want to sign the salon up for a Spirit Photography booth. I think Stacey will love that!"

Hamish and I agreed with her, then we went our various directions and I ended up intercepting the pizza delivery guy outside the inn.

Moonrise Manor's windows were all aglow against the

backdrop of a perfect autumnal night sky, and I took a moment to appreciate it before carrying the pizzas through the entry, where I also intercepted Aunt Millie.

"Pumpkin Squash!" (All the Wardwell Moms have a different pumpkin-related nickname for me, if you haven't noticed.)

"Hey, Auntie. Back out on the trails today?"

Millie pushed her auburn hair back from her face and dropped into a stretch. "You know it! Took a group of locals out. They all wanted to return for the meeting about the Harvest Festival, but I went back into the woods after I dropped them here. We have to take advantage of this weather before the rain starts!"

Aunt Millie's Witch sense can always tell when rain is coming. And snow. She can just sense it. She just so happened to be out of town on a hiking trip when winter barrelled in and ruined the Harvest Festival a few years ago. Without her to warn us, we never saw the shift coming.

"When do you think the rain will start?" I set the pizzas down on the check-in desk.

Millie popped up, pulling an arm over her head in another stretch. "I'd say before dawn." She started jogging in place. "I'm going to head out for a run before I'm stuck inside for days." Darting forward, she gave me a peck on the cheek. "Minerva is upstairs with Corbin waiting for you. She asked me to go grab my collection of comedy horror VHS tapes, so I'll be back."

I loved that my mom and aunts hadn't gotten on the uber-tech-savvy bus, either. "I guess it's a black comedy movie night then." No complaints here.

"You know your mother always has a theme! Toodles!"

I grabbed the pizzas and climbed the stairs, turning off

into the restricted wing that belonged to Grandma and Mom.

She was sitting on the couch in her living area with Sheriff Oliphant next to her. I'd say there was a safe distance between them if I were their chaperone, but their knees were perilously close to touching. Scandalous!

"Hey, guys," I said, dropping the pizzas on the coffee table in the only available space. Mom had laid out a plethora of dark comedy-esque snacks like hummus piped into a skull bowl to look like brains and a dark punch with floating gummy eyeballs. "When did you have time to do all this?"

"There is always time for assembling snacks. Sit, Pumpkin." Mom patted the spot on her other side. "Let's talk about the serious stuff while we wait for Millie to get back with our movies."

"I think you should start, Blair," Sheriff said, leaning back. I noted that his knees had moved away from Mom's quite swiftly upon my entry. "Mrs. Cobblepot told me you stopped by and sounded distraught."

I kicked off my shoes and curled up. "Boy, have I got a lot to tell the two of you."

"Did you get to talk to Anon?"

"No." I frowned and grabbed a chocolate-dipped strawberry ghost. "Tom wouldn't let me in. He just said Anon didn't want visitors."

Sheriff Oliphant grunted. "Did they ever let you in, Minerva?" Somehow I felt they'd had this discussion before I arrived, but were re-having it for my benefit.

"No," Mom said around a swallow of her eyeball punch. "I only went the two times you caught me. The first time, they acted like they weren't home or didn't hear me knock.

The second time, Tom answered the door and took the goodie basket, but wouldn't let me in."

"What are those two up to?" I said more to my strawberry than anything else and grabbed a soda.

"I don't know," Mom chimed. "But I did send a listening moth down the chimney and laced the truffles and muffins with truth serum."

I spit out my drink.

"Minnie!" Sheriff Oliphant chastised. "Tell me you didn't."

Mom looked offended at *him,* and I choked back a laugh. "I most certainly did. Do you want this solved or not, Corbin?"

"I want it solved, but in a legal manner. I could have sent a bug in there myself, but we have laws against these things."

"*You* have rules against these things as a man of the law," I piped up. "Those do not apply to us."

"Blair, it's just as illegal for a civilian to bug someone's house as it is for an officer. And what if they smash the moth with a swatter or set it free? Then what?"

"What I'm hearing is that you are interested in what intel Mom might gather."

Sheriff Oliphant rubbed at his temples. "*Wardwells.*" He spat it almost like a curse and Mom and I both chuckled. "What are you going to do if those two boys are in there at war with one another because you've dosed them into telling each other all their roommate and friend peccadilloes? Did you think of that?"

"Of course I did. If they get mad enough at one another, one might snitch."

"I can't..." He trailed off, lips pursed and scratching at his beard in irritation. "Blair, tell me you have something more lawful." A glare was tossed in Mom's direction and she shrugged, back to sipping her punch, unbothered. She even caught one of the gummy eyeballs in her teeth and squashed it.

I perked right up. "I do have info!" I proceeded to tell Mom and Sheriff all about my potion, the trails it revealed to me, and my thoughts on Art's shop being the missing link.

"I agree," Sheriff said when I was done. "If the trail led to the alley behind the bakery and you found spots of blood near the café, we can look into the idea of the perp going through Art's to get to the front of the bakery."

"Didn't you say the trail in the alley went cold, though?" Mom questioned me, her brows furrowed. "If the perp went through Art's, why would the trail stop at the café? Why the blood?"

I'd mulled over this quite a lot through the evening, but it wasn't until I began talking that it really came together in my mind. "The second trail in the park went cold, too. My hypothesis is that the other trail belonged to someone who shifted in the woods. That could mean the one that led to the alley was someone who shifted as well. Since I didn't know what race of creature to look for, it wasn't in my intention while creating the spell." I lolled my head from one side to the other. "Or they hopped in a car. I didn't think about considering vehicles in the spell, either."

Sheriff Oliphant appeared to be deep in thought. "Did you save any of the potion?"

I nodded.

"I'll come get some in the morning and repeat the spell, see what I can find." He stood and squeezed Mom's shoulder. "I'll see you ladies tomorrow. And Blair, steer clear of the Dread Monster until I can look into that blood you found. I don't like that it was behind the café."

I swallowed hard but made no promises. I couldn't get my mouth to form the words.

"Oh," he said, like he'd just remembered something and saved me from responding. "One more thing. I did get the report back from the county coroner. No name yet, but our John Doe was a Golem."

I was speechless still, but for an entirely different reason.

"That will make it almost impossible to figure out who he was," Mom said, thinking along the same lines as I was. "He could have been parading around as anyone."

"True," Sheriff agreed, "but even Golems die in their given form."

Sheriff left, and I couldn't stop thinking about the sparrow tattoo. Golems can take any form they'd like, but this man had chosen to tattoo his truest form.

When Aunt Millie arrived with the movies, I slipped the first tape into the old VCR and tucked my thoughts of murder away for later.

Mom and I watched movies and ate enough snacks and pizza to make us sick before I fell asleep on the sofa, my head in her lap. Exhausted as I was, there was no deep sleep for me. It was fraught with nightmares of Golems changing into the faces of the people I love.

CHAPTER 16

R ain sluiced down the glass of the circular, third-story window, the woods beyond a study in gloom.

I'm naturally a pretty upbeat kind of Witch who enjoys keeping busy, but I can also *really* get down with a cozy day indoors rotting with a good book.

Puck and Beetle were both curled up in my lap where we sat in the window seat, and Chester was glowing translucent in the curve of the window sill. In my black mug with little yoga skeletons all over it, I had a delicious brew from my stash of *Stonewood* coffee beans. And I was nearing the halfway point of the newest book club read. I'd even brewed a potion of cloves, orange peel, cinnamon, and nutmeg that was simmering in a cauldron downstairs, the aroma wafting through the entire cottage.

Aunt Millie had been right, the rain began by sunrise two days ago and had not stopped since. Yesterday, it was such a torrential downpour that almost no one left their house or opened their businesses up. This morning wasn't much better, but Millie called and said it should let up to just a drizzle by mid-afternoon. This was welcomed news because Maggie was getting stir crazy and I'm pretty sure Bill Winslow had called every Gloam Hollow resident five times to remind them what a crunch we were in for the Harvest Festival. He was not on speaking terms with Millie at the moment, as he claimed she should have informed him of the rainy spell *before* news of the festival went out.

Not being on speaking terms with Bill was kind of a goal in life, so Millie had not felt inclined to inform him the rain was going to let up. I, however, was excited to head into *The Copper Cauldron* after lunch.

Thinking of work took me out of my cozy mode and I gently urged the sleepy kitties off my lap. There was a smattering of responses, but I didn't bother translating from cat. I already knew they weren't kind words.

As I dressed in olive trousers and a ribbed sweater the color of cinnamon, I ticked through my checklist for the day.

First things first, I needed to locate my umbrella, but I could just use a summoning spell for that. Next, I wanted to ask Hamish if I could borrow his laptop and look at some more of Kat's articles on the news blog—see if anything stood out that might have lured the wrong type of tourist to The Hollow. A little research under my belt—oh! I needed a belt for my outfit—I'd head to the apothecary and get started on my Harvest Festival decorating.

Since the rain was interfering with all the plans, Bill had asked Ms. Lilly to send out a magic post to everyone who had not yet signed up, and those of us in that category selected our themes. My chosen theme was Classic Murder Mystery.

Mom said it was too on the nose, and she was right, but

you couldn't have paid me to change it, even though I could use the money if you did.

I slipped on my black galoshes and trotted down the stairs to the kitchen. Hamish was there at the counter, eating a treacle tart and typing away at his computer.

"What are you working on?"

He brushed some crumbs off his morning coat. Only Hamish would wear a morning coat in the kitchen without planning to be somewhere fancy. "I'm typing up the Harvest Festival plans for both the library and *Spellbound*." He swallowed a bite. "Mom was by earlier and said she offered to help too many people get their places decorated because of the time crunch and needed help with the boutique. The library didn't submit a theme early enough last year and we got stuck with barnyard animals."

I chuckled, snagging a bagel and spreading on some cream cheese. By '*barnyard animals*,' Hamish meant Petting Zoo. "I remember. How long did it take to get all the hay out?"

"Three weeks. I'm not doing that again." He gestured to his superb clothes. "Do I look like the sort of Warlock who handles animals?"

"Hey, you do pretty well with the cats." A thought occurred to me and I squinted at him, pointing my butter knife. "You've been cleaning out the cat boxes as promised, right?"

"Sure." Suspiciously fast, he grabbed his laptop and headed up the back stairs. "I'll be in the tree!"

I sighed and sat in Hamish's vacated seat to eat my bagel. Without his laptop, I was going to have to head to the library and hope someone had opened it today. Kids started back to school a couple of days ago, surely they hadn't closed *school* for the rain, and I figured students would need access to the library, right?

Once my bagel was consumed, I slipped on my clear raincoat (what's the point of a cute outfit if I have to cover it up?), and pulled on my brown leather backpack. Sure, I could spell the rain to not touch me as I walked, but I preferred not to use that kind of magic. There's something to be said for experiencing nature and life in the way it comes at you, without forcing it to be something else or some other way. I did, however, summon my Witch hat and umbrella, and made my way out into the rain.

The downpour was downpouring and I was soaked. Why did I leave the comfort of my reading nook again? Oh, yeah. A murder.

The square was deserted, as was to be expected, but I did see the lights on in *Stonewood* and a handful of other businesses. I jogged up the steps of the library, shaking my umbrella out once I was under the cover of the portico, and elected to leave it outside the door next to two others. No one wanted soggy carpets or books.

The other umbrellas were a positive sign and I found the door unlocked, open to the public. Some wise library employee had placed a coat rack just inside and I shucked off my raincoat, depositing it on a hook. After such a long, hot, and dry summer, little things like hanging a coat on a hook were pure bliss to me.

I recognized most of the faces I passed and said my cordial hellos on the way to the closest nest of computers. No one was there, so I took a seat and clicked the appropriate buttons to get to Kat's news blog. This time, I saw there was a drop-down menu that separated articles into categories. Conveniently, one category was: *Interesting Happenings In The Hollow*.

"Wish I would've seen that last time," I grumbled to myself. It would've saved me hours of website meandering. Oh well, we trust the process, right? Await the serendipity.

I clicked the category and let out a little gasp. Serendipitous, indeed! The first article—the most recent, published ten days ago:

MYSTERIOUS NEW CAFÉ OPENING IN GLOAM HOLLOW: WHO IS THE ANONYMOUS OWNER WHO SHIPPED IN HIS OWN BUILDING CREW?

The article detailed all the peculiar happenings of the café before we knew it was Aramis Hawthorne opening it. Kat speculated that it could be a secret chain restaurant, infiltrating The Hollow. She'd looked into the building permits with Bill Winslow, but only turned up a business name, Z Corp. It turned out Aramis didn't own the building like we thought, but, like most of us downtown, he was renting it. Aramis's landlord, the poor guy, was none other than Bill.

That explained why he didn't fight Bill too hard on some of the madness. Not only did he have a say over the café, but Aramis's apartment above it, too.

Near the bottom, the article had been updated five days ago—the day I met Aramis. It was an interview with Ms. Lilly and her speculation about the 'new guy' they now had a face for: a Dread Monster.

It was updated again the next day with one line. A link to an article titled: NEW MYSTERIOUS CAFÉ OWNER FINDS A DEAD BODY WITH A LOCAL WITCH

"*Peaches and pie crust!*" I Grandma-cursed. Oh, I am going to *throttle* Katarina.

I'd just clicked on the article when a message of glittering orange from Mom scrawled out in the air in front of the computer screen.

Sheriff's office, now. xoxo

I'd have to read Kat's article later. Closing out of the site, I threw on my backpack and rushed for the front of the library. Despite managing to wrangle my raincoat on over my backpack, I found the rain had nearly stopped when I stepped outside. Down to a slight drizzle, I didn't need the coat, but it was far too much effort to get it off now. I opened my umbrella and stepped out into the slick rain, hurrying to the sheriff's office. Worrying at my lip the entire way, I went over a hundred different scenarios for why he wanted to see me in such a rush. Each one was worse than the last.

I'd finally settled on the scenario where I was the one being arrested for murder and Sheriff Oliphant just didn't want to go out in the rain, so he asked the criminal's mother to contact her because she doesn't have a cellphone.

Perfect logic. But that's anxiety. She's a real treat.

When I bustled through the door, Sheriff Oliphant was right there, pacing back and forth.

"You really need a cell phone, Blair," he bit out.

"Hello to you, too." The struggle out of my raincoat softened him up until he finally sighed and helped me out of it. "What's got you in a tizzy?"

"I haven't been able to use the potion you sent over when the rain hit, so I've not had a chance to look at the potential perp trails, and the blood you saw has been washed completely away. I need you to walk me through what you saw in heavy detail now that the rain has let up."

Wilting, my tongue in cheek, I blurted, "You could have told me that before I got that stupid raincoat off." With a snap, I sent the raincoat home to the cottage—I didn't really need it, anyway. "Let's go, then!"

Despite our reason for going to the park, it was a delightful walk, all fogged gloom and dying leaves nestled beneath the trees to protect them from inevitable winter. "We won't head backward," I quipped as we walked.

"Pardon?" Sheriff looked at me sidelong, one hand resting casually on the gun I was fairly certain he'd never used outside a shooting range.

"The season." I pointed at the nearest tree we passed. "The leaves are gathering at the bottom of the trunks to protect the roots. Winter will be next."

There was a hint of a smile on ol' Corbin's face. "You have a keen eye, kid."

When we arrived at the park, it was deserted, what with the misting rain still lingering.

"This is where you saw blobs of green?" Sheriff Oliphant clarified as we stood staring at the spot Anon had been. I nodded and walked him through what I thought they meant, which one was clearly Anon's *blob,* and which were the swirling trails that led off toward the path.

"I couldn't spend much time looking at all of it with so many people in the park the other day, but it seemed like three trails altogether." I went and stood approximately where one had been. "This one seemed to engage with the other, presumably to attack Anon, but then it sort of moved back." I took a couple of steps backward. "It didn't converge with the other trail again until after Anon's went still on the ground."

Sheriff Oliphant was rubbing at his chin. "Then what?"

"Anon's trail went to that bench there, where he sat while the paramedic was looking at his injuries." I walked him past the benches. "The two trails went this same way, but one of them broke off in the woods." We walked that direction and I showed him where the trail had vanished as best I could recall. I cursed myself for not marking the spot for later—tagging a tree branch with a piece of cloth or something.

"And you're certain they were together?"

I started to say yes, but...now I wasn't so sure. How could I be? If I'd tracked my and Sheriff Oliphant's tracks they would have looked similar. "I don't know that I can be certain, but it seemed like it. They were around the same shade of green. The other tracks from earlier in the day or unrelated to the incident were much lighter because of timing or my intent when I crafted the spell."

We both stood in the woods, thinking for a moment before Sheriff nodded. "Alright. Show me what else you saw."

It was a tight squeeze down the narrow path with our umbrellas open, and all the leaves were slippery, but we made it. The trail spilled out onto the sidewalk beside the yellow house and I pointed across the alley street.

"I followed the trail across to the back of the shops." We crossed the narrow road and I stopped behind the café, showing him where I'd seen the blood spots.

Oliphant frowned down at a puddle of rain where the evidence had been. "Could it have been anything else? Ketchup, maybe?"

Suddenly, I felt like a huge fool. "It was too brown for ketchup, but this is a café. It could have easily been something else."

I was headed down a somber path inwardly, berating myself for acting like a detective when I had no business doing any such thing. Sheriff Oliphant sighed heavily and shook his head, the raindrops thunking onto his black umbrella.

I thought he would gently berate me as well, but he shocked me by saying, "I think you're onto something here, Blair."

I blinked at him, a sneaky raindrop sliding down my glasses.

"I'm going to see if Art will let us look around his shop. I need you to find out which family spelled his locks and when. Then I'm taking you for coffee."

I'd like to think I kept my excitement in check until he turned away to walk around the square toward Art's candy shop entrance. Then, I did a *small* jig before jogging to catch up.

Though ornery, Art is a kindly, elder Elf and is very seldomly cantankerous. However, no one who encountered him today would think of him as any of the former characteristics. He snipped and sniped at us relentlessly, but eventually let us do our jobs. Well, *job* was a liberal term for me, seeing as I was the only one of us not being paid.

Art's candy and souvenir shop is something stuck in the past in every way that is good, wholesome, and nostalgic. I don't think anything about it has changed since Gloam Hollow became a proper town. Every stone wall is still covered in glass jars of different candies in every size, shape, and color, each boasting a collection of plastic bags to fill to to your heart's desire. The only price for the candy was by weight, and it had always been that way. You could leave Art's spending hundreds of moonstones or hardly any—

there was something for everyone at every budget. The center of the shop, however, was littered with tables of Gloam Hollow souvenirs. Snow globes, bronze gazebo miniatures, even a figurine of Balthazaar, the skeleton who walks around the square in summer with the candy shop cart. (None of us know how Balthazaar walks around as a skeleton, but none of us question it, either.)

Once Art was done grumbling and went to sit behind his counter, Sheriff Oliphant walked slowly around the shop, surveying every inch carefully. I watched him for a while before beginning my own task, studying what he was doing and deciding if I noticed anything out of the ordinary. Aside from the back and front locks having a vague imprint of magic, I hadn't seen anything peculiar.

Without mentioning the magic I noted to Oliphant, I followed Art to his office to verify my discoveries first. Sheriff would likely have picked up on the same thing I did, but two heads were better than one.

Art closed me in his office with a vague threat of never being allowed in his shop again if I messed anything up. I didn't know what had gotten into the Elf, but I was glad when he left me alone.

Art was a pretty organized guy, but he'd been open so long that even once I found the correct drawer of files, it was *years* deep. That's when I remembered the front of the shop. *Gloam Hollow Candy & Souvenirs est. 4096.*

"Bingpot!" I rifled through files from the purchase and opening of the store with no luck. Finally, in the last file in that drawer, I found a sepia photo of a very young Lillian Tuttle, cutting the ribbon with Art. I snatched up the photo and ran out to find Sheriff Oliphant. He was bagging something when I approached, a red sticker with EVIDENCE stamped across it on the bag.

"What did you find?" I asked.

"Probably nothing," he said, sliding the bag into his pocket before I could make out what it was. "Find anything?"

I held up the photo. "I felt the magic on the locks, too. It had Lilly Tuttle's signature in it, but it was fuzzy—a little off."

Sheriff nodded. "I noticed that, too." He took a brief look at the photo before dipping his chin and turning to the Elf. "Arty, we're going to get out of your hair, bud."

Art grumbled something and swatted his hand through the air like we were pesky flies.

I watched Sheriff Oliphant study Art for a moment. "Is he alright?" I whispered.

Sheriff shook his head, just a small movement. "I don't know, darlin'. Old age might be getting to him." He started to turn toward the door and I followed, but then he stopped. "Hey, Arty." The cantankerous man looked up from his newspaper. "You remember that fishing hole you used to go to with my Pa?" Art squinted at him. "What was it called again?"

Art sat for a second, his face screwed up in thought, and when he spoke again, his kindly nature had returned. "You know, I can't remember, son. The old memory isn't what it used to be. You two have a lovely day, now. Looks like the sun is finally peeking out."

We both turned to look out the front windows of the shop. Sure enough, the rain had stopped and the sky was a mixture of gray clouds and slivers of sunshine.

"Thanks, Art." Sheriff waved. "I'll give you a call if I think of the name of that fishing hole."

"Please do. And Miss Wardwell, take one of those candy sticks you liked so much when you were a girl, the watermelon."

"Thanks, Art. You've been a big help." We waved and I snagged one of the watermelon candy sticks, shoving it in the side pocket of my backpack for later.

Aramis

The bell above the café door jingled. I was in the middle of counting plate inventory to ensure we'd received all I'd ordered, and whoever it was that walked in was going to have to wait. Henry had already interrupted my counting twice. Apparently he wanted to have a chat with Steven, who couldn't see him, and if I had to be the middleman one more time, I was going to scream.

"*Psssst.*" Cold air made the hair on my arms stand up as Henry floated beside me. "It's the sheriff."

Moving to a small town was supposed to *help* my mental health. I set my thrice ruined sheet of tally marks down and looked up. "What can I do for you, Sheriff?"

He strolled up, looking a bit smug, but I could see the concern at the edges of his eyes. This man might be my elder, but he hadn't seen half of what I had. In truth, I felt bad that I scared him so much. With a purposefully slow and steady hand, Oliphant set a baggie marked EVIDENCE on my bartop and slid it until it almost touched my fingers. "Want to tell me why I found a long, green hair in Art's candy shop after a man turned up dead near it and he claimed it had been broken into?"

I almost laughed. "That's a reach. Even for you, Oliphant."

"Is it? You don't strike me as the candy type. Why were you in Art's?"

"Since we're speculating here, maybe I've never been in Art's shop, or maybe I have and just wanted a Gloam Hollow souvenir to send to my mother." I pushed the evidence baggie back toward him. I'd seen all I needed to see of it.

"Yeah?" He leaned over the bar. I kind of like the guy, I really do. "And where does your mother live, Hawthorne? Because I can't seem to find any information on you."

I couldn't help the smile that curved my lips this time. Kenny had done his job well, erasing me. "You know I'm not the only one in this town with green hair."

"And the blood behind your café?"

I was on the verge of laughing. He was trying, I could give him that much. "Unless I'm under arrest for something, you can see yourself out."

Word of advice, my friends, never talk to the cops. You don't have to.

The evidence bag crinkled as Oliphant fisted it. "I'm watching you, Dread Monster."

"Hope you enjoy the view, Sheriff." I winked at him and he left, seething.

CHAPTER 17

Blair

"Kat said she swooped down and *sat* on the clocktower! Sat on it!"

"Mags, she would have crushed the entire square. There is no way," Hamish scoffed. "She's a massive *dragon*."

I heard this hushed argument as I came down the stairs, following the scent of coffee and muffins.

"You two should stop reading that girl's articles unless it's to mock them mercilessly."

"*Mom!*" Hamish said at the same time I stepped off the last step saying, "*Auntie!*"

"What?" Moira looked genuinely perplexed by our censure and took a bite of muffin. "I wish Minerva wouldn't send me on bakery errands," she said around a mouthful. "I have to fit into the new clothing line for winter." After one more bite, she tossed the rest of the muffin down with a muddled shriek of frustration and walked out. The sound of her heels clicking on the floor faded away until we heard the front door slam shut.

"Weeeelllll," Maggie said looking at me and wiggling her eyebrows, "are you looking forward to tonight?"

Ah, yes. *Tonight.* The taste-test/soft launch of *Spectre Café.* I was wholly undecided about how I felt about it. "Sure." I picked up a muffin and sniffed—apple crumble.

The rest of breakfast passed in typical fashion: muffins, coffee—tea for Hamish—general argument, and an agreement about dinner plans. Seven o'clock at *Spectre Café.* I had plenty to do that would keep my mind off an evening that could be disastrous or delightful. First, I wanted to start getting *The Copper Cauldron* set up for the Harvest Festival. Sure, it was almost a week away, but I like to be prepared, and the sooner I get it done, the sooner I can help anyone else who needs it. There's bound to be a fight over how we plan to decorate the cottage, too. There always is.

Apparently, Hamish somehow thought he was in charge of our theme and he wrote down 'Witches' on the sign-up sheet like a buffoon. We might as well just hand out plastic cauldrons and pumpkin spice lattés at the door because it didn't get any more Basic Witch than that.

Eventually, we went on our way to our various destinations. (In case you were wondering, I opted for checked tweed trousers and a brown cable knit sweater; brown leather platform casuals for the shoes.)

The pumpkins from our dear Autumnal Lady of Magic had cropped up absolutely *everywhere* and the walk to the apothecary was breathtaking. Relishing the crunch of leaves beneath my feet and my maple cinnamon latté from *Stonewood*, I was in perfect Harvest Festival harmony.

I planned to drop off my things at the shop, then head

into *Goodman's Grocery* to load up with everything they had to fit my theme of Classic Murder Mystery. The grocer was more like a general store and never had a ton of options, so I'd also need to scoot over to Lula-Ray's Party Barn.

For reference, yes, it's a barn.

When I passed the café, I noticed Aramis had finally taken down the paper over the windows and Ms. Lilly was gawking. "Hi, Lilly."

She jumped half out of her skin. "Oh, you scared me to death. I was just over at your mother's bakery, dropping off a decoration she wanted to borrow."

It had been just about four days exactly since the knock-out fight of Wardwell versus Tuttle at the town meeting. My prediction of them all being friends again within a few days had been right on the money.

"He's done a good job in there," Ms. Lilly went on, saying what she really wanted to be talking about. "Nice looking fellow, isn't he?"

I laughed and patted her on the back. "Easy, tiger."

"I'm married, not dead, honey. What do you know about this Dread Monster?" She tossed her chin in the direction of the café.

"Um... Not much..."

Now was as good a time as any to prod Ms. Lilly about the magic used to spell Art's locks the day he opened the candy shop.

"Do you happen to recall the day Art opened *Gloam Hollow Candy*?" I tried to sound casual, pausing to sip my drink. "I saw an old photo of you and Art cutting the ribbon together."

"Is that so?" She was still watching Aramis curiously. "I

don't recall, dear. That would have been a long time ago. I must have been just a teenager."

I started to ask her if she remembered spelling the locks at all, but she said, "Who's he talking to?"

I looked from her confused face through the window to where Aramis was arguing with what probably looked to her like the wall of eclectic coffee mugs hanging on hooks. "Wait, you can't see Henry the ghost?" I asked Lilly.

"Oh!" She laughed. "Henry! I forgot about that cheeky ghost. No, I can't see him."

I looked at her, my brow furrowed, but she waved a hand dismissively.

"Magic and the Sight differ from Witch to Witch, you know."

"Yeah, I suppose so."

Ms. Lilly said goodbye and headed back up the sidewalk, ending my questioning. I was too distracted by what was happening inside the café to even notice.

Aramis

"Henry! If you poke your head up through my apartment floor again while I'm showering, I'm going to find a way to wring your neck!"

"I didn't know it was the bathroom!" the ghost argued back. "When I was alive it was the *roof,* and I wanted to see the sunrise!"

"You're telling me you've been haunting this building for who knows how long and you didn't know there was an apartment up there?"

"No! And now, I'll never be able to clean my ghostly eyeballs of your bare b—"

Nope. I lifted my hair wrap before I could reconsider it. A viper slithered loose, carefully aimed at only my intended target. Mid-sentence, Henry turned to translucent stone. "Ah," I said to myself, instantly relaxing. "That's better."

The viper morphed back into a dreadlock and I tucked it away, then went to the kitchen to begin preparations for tonight.

Blair

I didn't know whether to laugh or scream. Henry was frozen as a block of spectral stone, one finger pointed at where Aramis had been standing, his mouth in the middle of forming a word. I couldn't hear what they'd been saying, but Henry had clearly been asking for it. Should I go in? Leave them be?

I settled on juggling my cup of coffee and a piece of paper from my bag, jotting a quick note that I slipped under the door of the café for the two of them to find at their leisure. When I stood up from sliding in the note, I saw Henry's stone form burst into a million shards and coalesce back into a specter that raced through the wall into the kitchen, face set in a yowl.

Shaking my head at the two of them, I went on my way.

This time, Beetle was the one in my shop when I unlocked it, up on the highest shelf eating a plant. I shooed her down, and she curled up in front of the hearth, so I lit the fire for her. "Why exactly do you three keep ending up here?"

The black cat gave me a look of quiet disdain that she'd learned from Hamish. She meowed and meowed, so much so that I had trouble translating, but I got the gist: Albis and Puck have been fighting over who gets to snuggle with her.

I interjected with, "Oh, dear," and "Oh, my," at appropriate intervals as she went on and on.

Beetle could not be bothered with their showmanship, so *'her Hamish'* has been sending them to my apothecary so she might have some *'peace and quiet.'* However, today, she felt like getting out of the house, so Hamish sent her here instead, leaving the boys to—and this is a direct quote—*'rot at the cottage.'*

"Well, good for you, Beetle. That plant you ate was poisonous, though. So you're going to need to go throw up."

She blinked at me.

I let her out back and groaned when she trotted down the sidewalk and around the corner. I did not have time for a cat who needed a specific place to throw up. Eventually, Beetle selected the trash behind *Toil & Truffle*. I had to give her credit for not just up-chucking on the sidewalk...

I looked up and saw Sheriff Oliphant knocking on the door of the yellow house behind the bakery. He was probably asking if they saw anything the night of the murder and I made a mental note to check in with him.

For now, I needed to head back out to see what I could gather from *Goodman's*.

The store was crowded with others finding what they wanted for their own Harvest Festival setups and stocking up on groceries they weren't able to get during the last couple days of torrential rain. I did manage to snag some file folders, baggies, and red markers to make evidence props, as well as some generic punch cups and Hor d'oeuvres plates. Very not fun stuff, but it was a start.

I lugged my bags back across the square and found someone had been in the apothecary. I distinctly remembered locking it. We'd all been better about doing so since the murder... Tingles shot up my arms and I dropped the bags. There was something on the counter.

Rushing over, I found it was a paper coffee cup with the *Spectre Café* logo on it—contents still very hot by the feel of the side—and a note. I almost couldn't breathe. Could Aramis really get through spelled locks? Had he been the one in Art's?

I opened the note with shaking fingers. A message in tight, manly script somewhere between cursive and kindergarten, read:

Wardwell,

Thanks for your note to Henry. He seems to respect you and has agreed he will not sit on the steps to my apartment anymore. It's a start. I'll have to tell you about the rest of his antics tonight. Enjoy the coffee, I know you usually have a cup around this time.

Let me know what you think. I tried something new.

Aramis

PS your cat let me in.

"Beetle!" She awoke from her perch on a bookshelf, bleary-eyed. "Did you let Aramis into my shop?"

Her mews were haughty at best. *He's handsome, darling, and he was bringing you a lil' treat.* She laid her head down on her paws and closed her eyes again. *We ladies have to stick together.*

"But how?"

Her kitty sigh was ridiculous. *You let Hamish through your locks, and I'm an extension of him as his familiar. Keep up, Witch.*

"I ought to send you home to the boys."

Beetle lifted her head. *You wouldn't!* she meowed.

No, I wouldn't. I was secretly pleased she'd let Aramis in. And that he'd noticed my coffee addiction. Or was that a red flag?

I shook my head. I'm going with green flag.

Men who bake pies and bring you brunch and learn how often you drink coffee don't murder people, right?

Yikes, that made him sound very murderer-y.

I popped the lid off the cup and sniffed. Between general Witchery, Mom, and Aunt Millie, I knew my spices well. Immediately, I could detect cinnamon, cardamom, cloves, and ginger.

"Mm, chai," I whispered to the dark, swirling liquid with just a hint of froth on top. But the coffee scent was strong, too.

I took a sip and the flavors burst across my tongue in what I can only describe as pure autumnal perfection. I put the lid back on and took another sip. There was one flavor I couldn't quite pinpoint, something that gave it an extra edge. Even so, my Witchy sense was not indicating anything sinister, only scrumptious.

It was not deadly coffee, so green flag. Definitely giving Aramis a green flag for this one.

I retrieved the bags I'd tossed down and unpacked them, then I took my delicious coffee and made my way to the

Party Barn, leaving Beetle with strict instructions not to let anyone in this time.

The trip there was a massive success, but it took ages because everyone was also there, like they'd been at the grocers. The mad rush to prepare for the Harvest Festival was well underway. Stands were cropping up all over town with various themes and carnival-style games. Booths were being built, floats constructed, and hay bale mazes set out.

By the time I made it back to the apothecary, the sun was setting and Beetle had apparently been magicked home. Too tired to consider doing any more with the decorating, I locked up and headed to Wardwell Cottage.

On the way, I saw Lacuna hard at work outside Stonewood, hanging streamers and giant trees she'd made out of thick craft paper. "Blair!" she said cheerily when she saw me, almost falling off her ladder.

"Woah, there." I sent magic darting out to steady her ladder, and another vine of it to hold the top of the paper tree that was about to fall on her.

"Whew." She climbed down and wiped her forehead. "Thanks." Arms spread as wide as her grin, she gestured to the front of the coffee shop. "What do you think? I went with Apple Orchard for my theme! We're going to have apple bobbing, apple picking, and apple toss!"

"I love it!" And I meant it. Already, the place looked great. "Want a couple of real trees to pick apples from?"

Lacuna's eyes went wide. "That would be perfect."

"I'll come put in a couple the night before."

She gave a little hop and wrapped her arms around my neck. "You're the best."

"It's my pleasure. Hey, have you heard from Anon at all?"

Lacuna's face fell. "No. He and Tom are being so strange. Maeve now, too."

"I've noticed." I didn't want to gossip or jeopardize the case at all, so I left it at that. "Let me know if you hear anything. I just want to make sure he's doing okay."

"I'm going to head over there after I lock up here. He hasn't been letting me in, but I keep trying."

"You're a good friend, Lac."

When I made it home, neither Maggie nor Hamish were there yet. They better not have forgotten our dinner plans because there was no way I was going alone. There was, however, someone up in my room.

"Hi, Pumpkin," Mom said when I entered. She chuckled behind her wine glass when I startled.

"Got any more of that?"

She pointed at my little side table. "It's a delicious rosé Moira brought back from her trip to the valley a few weeks ago," she said as I poured half a glass. I already knew what she was thinking when I saw her eyeing how little I'd poured. "Going somewhere tonight?"

I frowned at her. "How did you know?"

Mom shrugged and took a sip. "Mags told Moira this morning. So is this a date?"

"How could it be a date if my *cousins* are coming, hm?"

"I've seen stranger things."

"*Mama!*"

She tipped her head back and laughed, one of my favorite sounds. "I didn't mean anything like that. Well, what are you wearing?"

"Is this why you're here? To pester me about this dinner?"

"Partially. I also have intel back from my spy moth at Anon and Tom's."

I gasped and set my glass down, launching onto the bed and tucking my legs under me. "Lead with that next time!" I flailed my hands impatiently until her wine almost sloshed over the side of the glass onto my olive bedspread. "*Talk, talk!*"

"I didn't gather a lot. Unfortunately, Corbin was right about the truth serum. Those boys have been bickering like schoolchildren non-stop. So far, I've gathered that Tom was in the park that night with Anon, and they have a friend Anon no longer trusts, and this friend has come between Tom and Maeve."

"Do you think it's connected to the murder, then?"

Mom blew a breath past her dark red lips. "I really couldn't say. Just be careful going any further with all of this, Blair. It could be dangerous. Especially hanging around with that Dread Monster."

"Aramis is his name," I said a little too impatiently.

"Aramis," Mom amended. "Trust your Witch sense, Pumpkin Pie. That's all I'm asking."

"I will."

"Good." She set her glass on the nightstand and stood, clapping once. "Now, what are you wearing?"

CHAPTER 18

Dressed in an ankle-length pewter skirt (patterned with moths so tiny they almost resembled polka dots), and paired with a cropped, oxblood sweater and chunky boots, I ventured toward the *Spectre Café* with more than a few moths in my stomach.

Hamish and Maggie still hadn't shown up at home, and Mom was pushing me out the door by six-thirty so I wouldn't be late. That meant I was standing in front of the café more than fifteen minutes early. I couldn't very well just loiter on the sidewalk or half the town would ask what I was doing, nosy as they are. The best option was to go sit in the apothecary for a bit and read. But that decision came a second too late because Aramis walked through the door from the kitchen and saw me outside the front window.

Caught, I waved awkwardly and went in. A bell had been installed above the door and the café smelled *amazing* inside. It's always fascinated me that so many different foods can be cooked in a restaurant simultaneously and it smells good, but if you did the same thing at home, the scents would mingle in an unappealing way.

"Pick a seat, any seat," Aramis said by way of greeting. He was in full-blown café-owner mode in his *Spectre Café* logo tee under an unbuttoned blue plaid shirt. "Not that one," he stage-whispered when I picked a table. I laughed and he pointed out a longer one. "This is the best seat in the house."

I was even handed a menu once I managed to detangle from my purse and sit in a chair. "Fancy," I said with a cheesy grin—which he returned.

"How many will be joining you this evening?"

I had to stifle a laugh at his unusually proper tone. "Two."

Aramis laid out two menus and then gestured to a section of mine. "This is our drink selection if you'd like to peruse it, and I'll be back with a glass of water to get started."

"Thank you, sir." I tried to match his tone and he sputtered a laugh.

"Okay, enough of this. There's no way I can act so professionally every day."

"Drop the act, then." I shrugged and offered him a grin. "I can assure you this town will not reciprocate. We're more likely to throw pickles at your wall for getting our order wrong."

"Well, that is fine with me because I'm more likely to gripe at a customer for ordering incorrectly and throw their pickles at the wall myself."

A laugh bubbled up out of me at the thought, and I had to cover my mouth before I snorted. When I stopped the ridiculous laughter, Aramis was watching me, his eyes glittering. "Sor—" I started but stopped.

Aramis's mouth slid into a crooked grin. "There she is. No apologies." He tapped the table with two fingers. "I'll be back with your water."

When the kitchen door swung shut behind him, I let out a breath, eyes wide as I pulled at my sweater to fan myself. Twisting in my seat, I tried to look out the window to see if Maggie and Hamish were close, but it was pitch black out there, so all I could see was my own reflection and the misty glow of a lamppost.

Aramis came out a second later, carrying my water and a little ramekin of lemons and limes. I hadn't even looked at the menu yet, so I quickly read the drink names without reading their descriptions. There were sodas of course, coffees and teas, beers and wines, but the mixed drinks stole my attention: *Stormy Night, Smashing Pumpkin*, and *Spooky Black*.

"Your cocktails are themed!"

Aramis laughed. "I thought it would be fun to switch them out for each season." He lifted one shoulder. "Get with the Gloam Hollow spirit."

My stomach tightened in a knot. That sickening, lovely kind reserved for crushes. *Oh, brother.* I glanced outside again.

"I'll uh, take the Spooky Black," I told him, anxious to see what it looked like.

"Great. I love that one. Do you—" He rubbed at his beard. "Would it be weird if I made a drink for myself? Would that bother your cousins?"

It seemed like he knew it wouldn't bother me, and for

some reason that made me feel warm and fuzzy. Maybe I was the one who didn't need a drink. Or maybe I needed several. 'Twas a toss-up. "They would think it was weirder if you didn't."

Aramis nodded and ventured behind the bar counter. It felt strange to sit over at the long table by myself while he mixed the drinks, so I took my menu over to the bar and sat on a stool. He smirked at me and I dropped my attention to the wide array of food choices. Sliders, burgers, chicken pot pie... The list went on. There was a fairly innocuous breakfast menu—very *diner-style*—as well as a short dessert menu: churros, three flavors of pie, two flavors of cobbler, and *Toil & Truffle's Famous Donuts.*

The actual lunch/dinner menu, though, had some interesting options. "Cordon Bleu Quesadillas," I read off, eyeing him over my menu. "BBQ Chipotle Tacos, Loaded Shepherd's Pie Potato... Impressive, Dread Monster."

He stirred something into a glass that had to be mine because the entire drink was black as night. "I wanted to go for a unique menu, but also keep the small-town-diner feel."

"I think you nailed it."

"Thanks." He garnished my drink with basil leaves and slid it across the bar to me. "Gin, charcoal powder, crushed blueberries, fresh lemon, and ginger beer," he explained as I inspected it.

"It's so pretty I don't even want to drink it." I did, however, spin my little cocktail straw to watch the galactic contents swirl.

"I wanted something Witchy on the menu." He sounded so pointed when he said it that I thought I might panic and run.

Where were Maggie and Hamish?

Thank *Goddess*, Aramis changed the subject before I had to form a coherent response. "This one"—he began mixing another drink—"I call *Stormy Night* because of a legend my grandfather used to tell me."

As I watched him artfully mix spiced rum with ginger beer, lime, and bitters, he told me the tale of a captain who lost his love at sea and refused to ever disembark his ship, or even anchor it.

"Until one dark and stormy night," he said, his voice rumbly and mysterious—the mark of a master storyteller—"in the middle of fall when the waters were frigid, the captain's ship crashed onto an island." He began stirring charcoal into the drink until it turned a murky gray. "Alive, though barely, the captain crawled up the sand of the shore and lay there until he lost consciousness. When he awoke, a beautiful woman stood over him singing. It was the ghost of his beloved. He died that same night, and it is said they still haunt the isle together, hand in hand."

"*Crackers in a barrel*," I Grandma-cursed, sniffling. "What a beautiful story."

"It's a favorite of mine." Aramis took a sip of his drink and I did the same as he tapped my menu. "Pick anything you wish, Wardwell. I have just about everything already made in smaller portions. You can taste anything, everything, whatever you'd like."

"I am actually very interested in these quesadillas," I pointed them out on the menu.

"Coming right up."

He disappeared through the kitchen door and I sipped more of my drink—unsurprisingly, it was delicious—and wondered where he'd stowed Henry.

I heard the clattering of pans, followed by a string of

unique and *not* Grandma-Wardwell-style cursing. Drink in hand, I rushed around the bar and into the kitchen. "Are you okay?"

A tray of pies had crashed to the floor, leaving a pile of goopy mess. Aramis was crouched down with a rag trying to clean it up. "I was moving this tray out of the way and toppled the whole thing."

I considered using my magic to clean it up, but non-Witch people tend to frown on us interfering like that in most cases. Instead, I tried to find another way to be of help. "What's this over here?" I pointed to a pile of too-sticky dough.

Aramis looked up, his hands covered in cherry compote. "Ah, that's my ruined pot pie dough."

I pushed up my sleeves and washed my hands at the sink. I felt Aramis's eyes on me, but he didn't say anything. There was a towel next to the sink, so I carefully dried off my hands and went over to poke at the dough.

"Your butter was too warm. Maybe a little too much water as well." I looked over my shoulder to find him still crouched down, watching me closely as I added more flour to the dough, trying to save it. I cleared my throat. "Did you use ice water?"

Slowly, he stood with a handful of rags that looked like they'd been soaking up blood instead of pie filling. "I did use ice water, but someone has been messing with my thermostat, so the butter was too warm by the time I got to it."

"Who would mess with a thermostat? Oh... Henry?"

"Henry." He deposited the rags in the sink and washed his hands. For a moment, he looked lost, like he was looking for something, but it passed.

"Did you turn him to stone again?"

A deep, velvety laugh erupted from Aramis's chest and I felt heat lick up my neck. "Who told you?"

"I saw it!" I said, laughing too. "I watched you two argue this morning. That's why I sent the note."

"That ghost snuck in on me in the shower." His gestures grew animated as he spoke, the moths in my stomach fluttering uncontrollably.

I gaped at him, trying not to laugh at his expense. "Did you turn him to stone and lock him in a closet this time?"

Aramis gestured wildly with his hands toward the back storeroom. "Yes! That's exactly what I did. I figured out *one* viper stare only works for a few seconds, but *many* viper stares give me a couple hours of peace."

I fell into a fit of giggles, both of us laughing until I had tears in my eyes. Not thinking, I went to wipe my eyes and smeared flour all over my face.

"Here, let me help." Aramis closed the distance between us in two strides. He was so close so suddenly that I had to fight to breathe properly. Gently, he took off my glasses and set them on the counter. With warm, calloused fingers, he lifted my chin, using the edge of his shirt corner to gingerly wipe my cheek.

Dear Goddess, he smelled so good. Like cherry pie and comfort food and clean soap. I watched his eyes flick to my mouth before he swallowed hard. His thumb gently brushed my chin before he dropped his hand and stepped back.

"There you go. Right as rain." He smiled at me as he handed me my glasses. Then he moved to the stove and the spell was broken.

I sipped at my drink—guzzled is more like it—and

returned to my work resurrecting the pie dough. In a jiffy, I had it headed in the right direction.

"I suppose having a baker for a mother, you'd know your way around dough," Aramis said, breaking the silence as he stirred something that smelled amazing.

I grabbed the rolling pin and dusted it with flour. "Yep. I know my way around most pastries, but no one makes them like Mama." I caught my mistake and turned to him with wide, apologetic eyes.

"Ah, ah," he said. "Don't you dare say you're sorry."

I smiled, feeling my cheeks go pink, and started rolling out the dough.

"Do you ever use magic to cook or bake?" Aramis asked after a brief moment of companionable silence.

"No, I really don't. If Witches do that, all the food sort of begins to taste the same, like when a restaurant uses the same cookware to make all their food." *Bah*. I was really putting my foot in my mouth tonight.

But Aramis nodded, removing his skillet of what looked like pot pie mixture from the heat. "I know exactly what you mean." He set the skillet down on a hot pad and grabbed my wrist, pulling me to the back wall. There, he opened a door to a pots and pans closet. An *entire* closet full of them.

"They're labeled," I said in astonishment.

"Every food dish has its own cookware and utensils," he explained. "Steven and Kendall are a little overwhelmed by it, and I know I'll need to hire an official sous chef to keep up with all of this work, but you're exactly right. You can't keep the flavors from combining after using the cookware for a while. That is the big secret to serving delicious dishes for years to come."

"You're a little bit of a mad cooking genius, aren't you?"

He nudged me with his shoulder and I laughed.

The rest of the evening passed in easy conversation, cooking, and far, far too much food. We never did make it to the dining area—I'd all but forgotten it even existed. Instead, we crowded around the stove or the butcher block prep table, sampling dishes. At some point, Aramis dragged over stools and we sat across from one another eating and chatting about everything under the sun, plates littered around us. I couldn't recall the last time I'd had such engaging conversation. It was to the point I thought we'd never run out of things to talk about.

When the kitchen was an absolute disaster and we were beyond stuffed, Aramis brewed some of his delicious coffee. I watched him work in the first real moment of silence we'd had since I arrived, but it was the comfortable kind of quiet.

I had difficulty tearing my eyes from his toned forearms, sleeves rolled up as he ground the coffee beans and tamped them down in the portafilter. I couldn't tell what was my Witch sense and what was the moths in my belly, but all of it was wonderful.

The smile he gave me as he brought over two steaming cups sent the moths into a proper tizzy. We sat sipping the coffee and Aramis handed me a plate of churros. I took one and set it on my little dessert plate, but then thought better of the choice and grabbed another. He chuckled and I blushed.

"I'll never be one of those really *fit* girls," I said, biting into my churro, the cinnamon sugar dusting my fingers and lips. "I will always grab seconds and I will always have another piece of dessert."

"As well you should. What's life without enjoying good food and good company?" Aramis watched me, leaning over the table on his forearms, hands cradling his coffee mug as the steam coiled up toward those green eyes. "Besides," he said, his voice deep and rolling like thunder, "I like a girl who can eat. And I quite like your curves."

Sweet mercy, I almost choked on my churro.

Into the wee hours of the morning, Aramis insisted on walking me home. He blamed the late hour and a lurking murderer, sobering me right up. But the effect didn't last long. By the time I drifted off to sleep in the coziness of my fluffy duvet, I was on cloud nine.

It wasn't until I woke up in the morning that I realized Maggie and Hamish had never shown up. I stormed into Maggie's room so fast the door hit the wall.

"Wha–what happened?" she garbled as she tried to sit up, still mostly asleep.

"You didn't come to the café last night!" I accused.

Hamish shoved past me to sit in Maggie's lounge chair. "Took you long enough to realize." He blew on his tea, eyeing me.

"B," Maggie said, hands over her eyes and her voice scratchy, "we did show up. But when we walked in, the two of you didn't even hear the bell. You were laughing hysterically about something, so we peeked into the kitchen window and he was wiping flour off your face, looking at you like you were the only person who's ever lived."

I turned wide, accusatory eyes on Hamish and he was grinning like a wolf. "No way we were about to interrupt that." He shrugged. "So we went for Pho with the moms to talk about you two."

I buried my face in my hands and groaned.

The rest of that day was spent fielding questions around

town about my evening of leisure with *'the new Dread Monster,'* *'potential murderer,'* *'cute café guy.'*

Apparently, Ms. Lilly was to blame for this. Her entire response was: "The gossip knife cuts all ways, honey. I don't discriminate against who's on the other end of it, I just slice."

CHAPTER 19

Days passed by in a blur. Tourists were filing into Gloam Hollow in droves. *Moonrise Manor Inn* was over capacity, as were the two smaller inns in town and *Dewdrop Bed and Breakfast*. A special town meeting had even taken place mid-week to come up with a solution. Eventually, we'd landed on a few townspeople offering up spare bedrooms and setting up a campground in the park. This endeavor was covered by a magical tent that was part work of art and part nightmare, created by a joint effort of Tuttle and Wardwell Witches. We each spent an hour a day fortifying it from rain, and Mom slipped in a protection spell—what with a murderer on the loose. A couple of days ago, Aunt Millie had even taken three families up to some cabins on the mountain trails, and we'd all done the best we could.

Sheriff Oliphant had given me no new information on the murder case, but I had a sinking feeling in the pit of my stomach about it. Maybe the killer had already left town. Why would they stick around, anyway? What if we were too late?

Whoever the victim was, no one seemed to have known he was here, because still no one had come to claim him. It had eventually been decided that he would be buried in the Gloam Hollow Cemetery next week when the Harvest Festival was over unless someone showed.

I was as exhausted as everyone else, but just as exhilarated. We *lived* for this time of year.

Though the festivities weren't officially supposed to begin until tomorrow, today had already proven to be the busiest day yet and the sun had barely risen.

I was standing in front of *Spectre Café* with an armload of items to help Aramis decorate for the haunted café. Hamish and Maggie were due to meet us at any moment once they grabbed us all coffee from *Stonewood* (I was sure they would show this time), but there was a wrench in the works named Bill.

"You're not open yet, Aramis!" the mayor was shouting. "You can't keep serving food!"

And Aramis was shouting right back. "The permits are in place—*you* approved them, and I have food because I was supposed to *open* tomorrow. These people are knocking down my door, Winslow! They're hungry and I'm not going to turn them away."

We had not properly prepared for this many tourists. Sure, we had restaurants and things, and the inn had stocked up on food for their small restaurant as well, but even the grocer and his local suppliers were running out. Yesterday, Aramis had called in a special delivery from who knows where. Two massive trucks pulled into town, hardly fitting down the roads, and dropped off a load of food at the grocers. Then they split up and delivered some to

Spectre, some to Grandma's inn, and some to the park. Aramis had even helped Aunt Millie lug food up to the cabins.

Needless to say, we hadn't yet been able to get the haunted house ready and we were short on time.

"You don't have a permit to sell food in the park!" Bill was shouting again.

"I'm not selling the damn food, Winslow!"

"Bill!" I interjected, stepping between them. "Do you want to go feed all those people out of *your* pocket?" His face mottled and he glared between me and Aramis. "I didn't think so. Now, don't you have more important things to worry about?" I lifted up my bundle of stuff. "Because we have a haunted house to set up."

Bill stormed off just as Mags and Hamish arrived. "We come bearing the magical bean water!" Maggie declared, handing out cups of coffee.

Aramis thanked them profusely, looking like he hadn't slept in a week. There hadn't been much time for us to talk since the absolutely perfect night we'd spent together at the café, but every once in a while I caught him staring, and he always seemed to know exactly where I was at any given point in time when we were in the same area of town. Yesterday, I'd even arrived to find a moonblossom on the counter in the apothecary, and a note saying he'd like to properly take me out. Oh, and that Puck had let him in. I hadn't seen Puck around the shop, but it seemed the Wardwell cats were in the business of meddling in affairs of the heart.

Hours of gauze, skeletons, lighting, and one very large cardboard Vampire castle cutout later, I could hardly see straight. We'd gone more spooky and intriguing than full-on scary. The idea of terrifying a bunch of children that might wander in had been unanimously decided to be a bad idea.

"Wardwell," I heard Aramis say in a bemused tone that led me to believe he'd said my name at least three times already before I registered it. I'd fallen into a daze staring at a wall, deciding how to decorate it. When I turned to face Aramis, his face was torn between amusement and concern. "When was the last time you slept?"

"I could ask you the same thing."

He took the bundle of black, stringy cloth and gauzy spiderwebs I was holding with one arm and handed me another cup of coffee with the other hand. "Fair enough. Drink up or I'm sending you home for a nap."

I gratefully took a sip and used that opportunity to sit. Aramis went back to work on the entrance out front and three seconds later, Maggie came tearing through what used to be a dining area. One of the skeletons only half-hung from the ceiling knocked into her head and she spat a Grandma Wardwell obscenity at it before she detangled herself.

"B, Henry is acting like a primadonna, and now he refuses to talk to anyone else but you."

I laughed and stood, surprised to discover how stiff and sore I was. "He is the star of the show, after all."

When we found him, Henry was sitting on top of the stove, his chin on his ghostly fist, while Hamish was laid out flat on the butcher block table Aramis used to prepare food. If he saw that, we were going to have another ghost on our hands.

"Finally!" Henry perked up when he saw me. "Tell these heathens that I will not be made a mockery!"

Hamish groaned and sat up on his elbows. "All we asked

him to do was jump out and scare people that walk in. Slam a door or something."

"I am a specter not a poltergeist!"

"I don't even see the difference," Hamish shot back. "Can't you just be both?"

"Do you hear him, Blair?" I'd never seen Henry look so offended and he sort of *always* looked offended.

"I'm too tired for this," Maggie mumbled and walked out.

"Hamish, get your feet off the table." I smacked his shoe. "Henry, you agreed to be the star of this haunted café and that means you have to *act*." My very carefully selected word choices had their intended effect because Henry pulled his spectral shoulders back and lifted his chin. "Not everyone can see you," I went on, "so you might have to make a little noise. Really give them a good show. Rattle some pots and pans, sway a few skeletons."

Henry's confidence faltered. "I don't usually touch things. It takes a lot of energy..."

"What about when you mess with Aramis's thermostat?" I lifted one eyebrow at him.

"Snitch," the ghost spat, then straightened, his chin high. "That is different. I put my hand *into* the thermostat, and push at the little flicky thing that controls the temperature until it wiggles."

"Flicky thing?" Hamish snorted from the table.

"That's not so different. You can do it, I know you can," I encouraged him.

"Here." Hamish hopped down from the table and grabbed a pot, setting it on the stove next to Henry. "Try picking this up and slamming it back down."

It took several tries, but eventually, Henry lifted the pot, his face strained, and let go, the pot clattering to the floor.

"Oh, Goddess," Aramis said as he walked in. "Tell me you haven't taught him how to make noise now."

Hamish and I exchanged a pair of cringing looks.

"Uh, I gotta go." Hamish rushed out of the kitchen two seconds before Maggie yelled from the dining area, "Tape! I need tape!"

I dashed toward the back for more tape, but Aramis caught my arm and pulled me toward him. "Hey," he said, his voice so low and raspy that I struggled to pull sufficient air into my lungs. "Can we take just five minutes today? I know you're right here, but I'd like to spend real time with you."

I didn't even know what to say, not that I could have gotten any words out of my cotton-filled mouth, anyway. I wasn't used to dating at all—the pool of men in Gloam Hollow had always been shallow—but I definitely wasn't used to men who just came right out and said what they wanted and didn't *play it cool* (AKA, play it stupid.)

"I'd love that," I said honestly, and my reward was in the glowing smile he gave me.

"First chance we get."

"First chance we get," I agreed.

Alas, the likelihood of that chance wasn't looking good. When *Spectre* was decorated and locked for the day, Aramis commandeered a wheelbarrow that had been used by one of the local farmers to lug in hay for the mazes. He filled it with food stuffs and he and Hamish pulled it up the trails to the cabins in the woods. I wish with all my wishes that I could have gone to see Hamish lugging anything anywhere and traipsing through the woods in his loafers, but I'd been summoned to the inn to help Mom and Grandma finish up there.

"I thought they said the theme was Dracula's Castle," I said to myself when I walked in to find all the decor was very Vampiric and very Victorian, but feminine and not at all spooky.

"It's *Countess* Dracula's Castle now."

I turned to see Maeve in a turn-of-the-century ball gown of deep crimson and weepy, black lace. "You look incredible!" I said through an astonished laugh.

Aunt Moira trotted in behind her, bowing. "Thank you, thank you. Save your applause for the end of the festival."

Maeve rushed over and grabbed my hands, smiling from ear to ear. "Isn't it fantastic?"

All of her decorum had fled, and, it seemed, so had her strange behavior over the last week. Perhaps things with her and Tom had sorted themselves out. I didn't know where that left Anon or the attack on him, though.

"Moira is going to do my hair and makeup and Tina has written an entire script for all of us," Maeve gushed. "It's going to be incredible!"

"It sounds like it!" I couldn't help but be swept up in her excitement. There's something really beautiful about just seeing your friends *happy*, especially over seemingly small things. Life—real life—is buried in those small moments, and we miss them too easily waiting for the rare showstoppers. "I positively cannot wait to stop by your castle tomorrow night," I uttered in my most proper Vampire voice.

Maeve laughed at my attempt. "Looking forward to it. Okay, I have to go change out of this dress and hit the books again. This influx of visitors has our accounting all out of whack."

I found myself thinking as she bounded away that I was glad she'd stayed on at the inn. We'd begun working here as little sullen teenagers, sweeping floors and changing sheets, but ten years later, Maeve was running the books and managing most of the staff herself. It gave Mom and Grandma more free time as well to enjoy the spoils of all their hard work and to run the bakery.

"Hi, Pumpkin Pie," Mom said breathlessly when she entered the cleared-out sitting room carrying a crate of things. She set it down and brushed her hair out of her face. "In here, Andrew!" she called out into the hall.

Andrew came in carrying a very tall ladder. He smiled and nodded when he saw me, then followed Mom to set up the ladder where she wanted it. "Are you sure you don't want me to hang all this, Ms. Wardwell?"

"You're sweet, dear, but you're a guest. We only use guests for their muscles and we do the rest."

Andrew laughed at her joke and waved to me before leaving.

"Nice boy," Mom said to herself before addressing me. "I've heard quite a lot about *your* nice boy around town." She waggled her eyebrows at me and I laughed.

"What have you heard?"

We began pulling out decorations from all the crates and tubs around the room as we talked. "Oh, just that he's been seen all over the place making sure everyone has enough food. I heard he delivered to-go meals to several families last night and then went in and cooked Old Mrs. Flannigan a meal in her house after that."

My heart gave a little jump. I hadn't heard the part about

Mrs. Flannigan. She's a bit of a handful (Faerie, and not the sweet kind), but something told me Aramis hadn't had any trouble with her at all.

"He definitely doesn't shy away from feeding people," I said, then finished the thought in my head: even if he did shy away from most people for every other reason. "Any more talk of him being a suspect in the murder?"

Mom raised her eyebrows at me. "Depends who you ask, I suppose.

Not comforting. "What are we decorating this room for?"

"This will be Countess Dracula's ballroom." Mom beamed, holding up a lace tablecloth.

"Have you talked to Sheriff Oliphant in the last few days?" I asked after a few moments of decorating and chit-chat.

"You know," Mom stopped, frowning, "now that you mention it, I haven't. Corbin has been so busy with the murder case, and then all the drama around town with the festival, that I haven't even seen or heard from him in days."

"What's that look for?" Her frown had deepened, and she looked almost hurt. "Are you alright?" I pressed.

"I'm fine, Pumpkin." She shook her head and got back to work. "It's just a little strange I haven't heard from him is all. We've been talking every day lately."

That coil of dread in my stomach that had hidden itself away for a few days? It dropped back in place so swiftly that I felt a bit nauseous. "I'm sure he's just busy," I said to reassure Mom, but I was beginning to worry that something more serious had happened.

By the time the inn was fully transformed into Countess Dracula's Castle, it was past midnight. We were due to our respective booths and shops bright and early in the morning to entertain patrons and townsfolk alike once the parade was over. Thank Goddess, when I returned to Wardwell Cottage, Maggie had finished decorating and even had four *huge* cauldrons outside full of candy waiting for all the kids who would come by.

On the porch, there was also a very handsome Dread Monster, asleep on the porch swing.

He was so peaceful and he'd been so tired lately, that I decided to tip-toe past him and just let him sleep. I made it one step before he reached out and grabbed my wrist. "Don't you dare," he crooned, one eye open. "I've been waiting all day to spend time with you."

"Then shove over, Hawthorne."

The grin on his face made my heart flip.

"Did you look up that band I told you about?" he asked, his head leaning against the swing's chain.

I situated myself on the seat next to him, leaving an appropriate amount of space—but not too much. "I haven't had a chance to go to the music store yet, but I can't wait."

Aramis lifted his head, eyes sparking in the porch light. "There's a music store here?"

I laughed. "Yep. I'll take you." The words were out of my mouth before I realized how presumptuous it might be.

But he smiled. "I'd like that. However, I meant for you to look them up on the Interweb."

"Gag!"

Aramis laughed and I couldn't help but join in. "Right, right. You told me you hate technology, but there are good things about it. Like music and research and a site where you can have little digital boards of inspiration."

That got my attention. "Like a collage board?"

"Just like that. But instead of pinning or gluing magazine

cutouts of all your favorite outfits"—he nudged me—"it's all right there on the web."

I should have been embarrassed he'd inferred I had mood corkboards in my room, but I was intrigued. "Okay," I conceded. "Maybe, *maybe* I want you to show me that..."

Aramis laughed again. "I'll show you that website if you show me the music store."

"Another deal?"

"Another deal."

We were talking on the swing about all that had transpired between our stolen moments together over the last several days, and the next thing I knew I was waking up on the stairs, bobbing in someone's arms.

"Shh," Aramis whispered, "go back to sleep." The stairs creaked under our weight as he carried me, lulling me back to sleep.

CHAPTER 20

"Carried you!" Maggie squealed for the fiftieth time since we'd left the cottage. "He *carried you.*"

"I wish I could remember more of it," I grumbled, still half asleep.

"I wish we'd talk about literally anything else," Hamish grunted in similar fashion.

"You two are awfully glum for the best week of the year beginning today!" Mags held her arms out wide and spun on her toes, the two of us lagging behind.

She was right. The air was crisp and foggy, hundreds of people milled about in costumes, the leaves were piled up around the pumpkins littering the town, and the air even smelled of baked apples, cinnamon, and spice.

And I'd been *carried* up to my bed to be tucked in by the first guy I'd been interested in for ages.

A smile slipped onto my face and a little more pep slipped into my step.

"Oh, geez," Hamish griped when I joined Maggie arm in arm.

He was dressed in a lab coat, a wild shock of green hair sticking up all over his head, and Maggie was dressed as an old-fashioned photographer, a faux ghost bobbling around on her shoulder. I boasted the attire of a lady sleuth, done up in brown wool tweed, a matching deerstalker hat, a lovely cloak, and—of course—I carried my trusty magnifying glass.

By the time we'd reached the end of our tree tunnel road, we'd already seen Faeries dressed as Witches, an Orc dressed as a lumberjack, a group of people wearing various indiscernible costumes—you know the kind, they're either too clever to understand or they're too obscure to make sense of—and several little children in Witch, Elf, Vampire, or Werewolf garb.

We walked the rest of the way to the square together for coffee at the *Stonewood* Apple Orchard—the apple trees I magically installed were a huge hit—and watched the parade together. When it wrapped up, we all split to go our separate ways, vowing to meet back together in the afternoon when our duties were done.

Once fueled by a few sips of espresso, Hamish was much more cheerful and hopped off to the library, which had been decorated as a giant mad scientist laboratory. Mags bounded off to the salon—a spooky portrait station for the day—and I all but skipped to *The Copper Cauldron* to begin my first murder mystery session of the day.

I'd planned each mystery session to last twenty minutes, locking the door and using my assembled crowd for each round. Everyone received an envelope with their role, and we ate snacks, followed the clues I'd laid out, and eventually found a murderer!

To say it was a smashing success would be putting it lightly. We had hiccups occasionally and several spilled bottles of potions, but all in all, it was a blast. I even sold a good portion of my stock to out-of-towners, and a few books, too.

Once everyone began to assemble on the sidewalk around the green in anticipation of the carnival, I decided to end my murder mystery sessions there, so I could stop by everyone else's places for opening night, and enjoy the carnival myself.

I visited *Toil & Truffle* first, delighted to see Mom dressed up as a giant pumpkin and the patrons having the best time making adorable spooky treats. People of all ages were crowded around three long tables, a mess of sprinkles, frosting, and crumbs littering every available surface. Kids were leaving with frosting up to their ears, and parents murmuring things like, *'Here comes the sugar rush!'* before they bustled back out onto the sidewalk. I gave Mom a quick kiss on the cheek and snagged a spider cupcake and a ghostie truffle.

My next stop was Aunt Millie's *Broom & Blossom*, where she was dressed as none other than a Witch—the classically hideous kind. She was handing out brooms and patrons were decorating them with fall leaves, flowers, vines, and gems, then riding them outside to await the carnival opening. I waved at Millie and she rushed across the room, tossing me a broom she'd already wrapped with fall foliage. "Every Witch needs her broom, Pumpkin Squash."

I felt a little silly carrying my broom as I walked around dressed as a detective, but my fingers were already itching to grip it and fly up toward the moon. It had been far too long.

Maggie's was my next stop. Their Spectral Photographs Station at the salon was fun, but my mind was elsewhere, thinking of Aramis and why Sheriff Oliphant had been so silent about the case.

The stylists dressed me up in vintage clothing and I '*sat for a portrait.*' The camera bulb flashed, blinding me, and then they carted me to the side where I was handed a sepia printout of myself with a spectral glow above my head.

"This," Maggie's boss Stacey said dressed as a fortune teller, "is the ghost of a long lost love from a different life." She made appropriately spooky sounds and wiggled her fingers until we both laughed.

Cutting across the green, headed for *Stonewood*, I had to dodge all the stands and one very angry mayor in the gazebo, who shouted at me that '*the carnival is not open yet,*' and, '*why does everyone think they can do whatever they want today?*' I didn't know what had gotten into Bill, but then again, I never did.

I picked a few apples at Lacuna's and stored them under the counter for later, (hey, a basket of apples is heavy!) along with my broom. When I left there, I wanted to stop in *Spectre Café*, but we'd all agreed to go there together after the carnival.

Then, I made my way to Aunt Moira's *Spellbound Boutique* and watched as her (cute!) monster factory pumped out adorable costumes. Kids were laughing hysterically, gluing a thousand eyes on tie-dye shirts and Vampire fangs on Werewolf masks.

Moira caught my eye and jumped up from her cushy stool. Her measuring tape fanned out behind her as she ran over to me and whispered, "In my office, there's something for you." She winked and left me gaping.

Curious beyond belief, I spelled the lock to Moira's office open and retrieved a beautiful black and white box. In it was an absolutely divine trench-style olive peacoat. With it a note: *'You should be the first to wear my Dark Academia Collection, affectionately named: Blair.'* I wanted nothing more than to wear the beautiful coat, but I was still dressed as an investigator and we'd all planned to go to the carnival and haunted café in costume.

With only a couple more stops to make before coming back for the carnival, I could drop the box off at the cottage if I timed it right.

The library laboratory was *insane*. Everything was dry ice and shelves of beakers with specimens in them. There was even a giant—and I mean *giant*—chemistry set that looked more like a miniature amusement park ride, boasting gurgling chemicals in every color imaginable. Hamish was running around spooking people and handing out mini science booklets in lieu of candy.

When he saw me, he shifted his goggles up to his forehead and rushed behind the counter. "For you, my lady." He bowed like a perfect mad gentleman and handed me a booklet. "Did you hear Cory Tennenbaum proposed to Betty Tuttle at the gazebo?" he whispered.

I gasped and smacked Hamish with the booklet. "He did not!"

"I know!" He was just as giddy as I was. "They've surprised everyone. Bill didn't sanction the use of the gazebo, either, so he's all in a rage. It's a huge scandal."

I laughed. Bill's fit certainly made more sense. "Maybe as much of a scandal as Gloam Hollow has seen," I joked. Well, aside from the murder. That put a swift damper on my mood. Maybe I should stop by the sheriff's department on my way home...

With a last-minute decision after leaving the library, I decided to turn around and go up Hollow Hill to Countess Dracula's castle, instead, and skip the sheriff's department entirely. It was probably only decorated with two jack-o-lanterns and a candy bowl, anyway, and it wasn't likely Oliphant was going to give me any real information about the case. Or was it cases plural? I still didn't know.

Moonrise Manor Inn was crawling with people, the staff pulling them into dances and offering bubbly juice and cocktails. Mom rivaled Maeve in her Victorian dress, while Grandma was dressed as Countess Dracula's meek familiar. That was comical. Grandma Wardwell hadn't been meek a day in her life. I gave them all hugs and told them how wonderful everything looked, then went on my way. I debated pulling Mom to the side to see if she'd heard from Sheriff Oliphant, but my Witchy sense tingled—not a good idea. Mom deserved a night of fun without worrying about murder and what Corbin was up to.

By the time I left the inn with my coat box and science booklet in tow, I'd successfully pushed the murder case from my mind, at least a little. I rushed the box home, downed a cup of coffee—and burned my throat—then rushed back to the square just in time to meet everyone for the carnival.

Aramis never did show, but Maggie, Lacuna, Hamish, and I attempted to reach every booth, exhausted by the time we'd done it.

"I think I have hay in my underwear," Hamish groaned, and we laughed.

"I'll be snorting out apple-bobbing water for a week," Maggie added.

"You couldn't pay me to bob for apples," Lacuna laughed. "Everyone sticking their face in the same water and nipping at the apples?" She shuddered. "Too many germs!"

"You had apple bobbing in your own coffee shop all day today," I pushed her playfully.

"That doesn't mean I partook!"

We were all laughing and dodging sugared-up kids, enjoying the glow of the lights and our candied apples when Anon and Tom walked up.

"Hey guys," Tom said, but Anon held back.

We all just sort of blinked at them, at a loss.

"Uh," Tom finally broke the awful silence. "Mom said to stop by her shop for some spooky boba on the way to the haunted café. She made them special and offered freebies for you guys."

Aw, man. I think my heart cracked a little. I didn't know what these two had been doing, or what madness their new *'friend'* had gotten them into, but Tom was at least trying to mend the rift.

"That sounds amazing," I said cheerfully. Picking up on my lead, Hamish and Lacuna said similar things.

"You guys are coming with us, right?" Lacuna smiled at them, but she was really only looking at Anon. I could almost feel the sadness in her, despite her demeanor. She was as close to Anon as I was to Maggie and Hamish. I would be devastated if there was such a chasm between us.

"Yeah," I jumped in, laying it on perhaps too strongly by looping my arm through Anon's. "Let's go. Bobas then haunted café."

Anon pulled out of my grasp and my stomach dropped

as quickly as Lacuna's smile did. "I'm going to head home." He turned and walked away, lost to the crowd before any of us could stop him. Tom watched the direction he'd gone, his face drawn.

"You're still coming, right?" Lacuna tried to smile again, but it fell flat.

"Yeah. Yeah, I'll come." His voice sounded tired and I couldn't help but feel terrible. Maybe the evening of fun would cheer him up some.

We walked as a group to the ice cream and boba shop. Tom and Hamish chatted quietly as we girls gushed over the adorable bat bobas in our variously colored milk teas. Mine was orange, Maggie's was green, and Lacuna's was purple. They all had a mystical swirl to them that smelled of magic, and I wondered if it was a Tuttle or Wardwell who'd stopped in to spell Linda's recipes.

With one sip I knew it was Grandma's magic, and the comforting conjury settled my nerves.

Walking into *Spectre Café*—nay, *The Haunted Café*—was like walking into a different universe. Despite being one of the people who had a hand in setting the place up, the black lights and eerie darkness Aramis had added after we left yesterday were the perfect touch.

I sensed and saw Henry coming a second before he popped up, and he scared the daylights out of everyone in the vicinity. Some because he came out of nowhere, others because they couldn't see him, only feel the coolness of his presence or hear the horrible noises he was making. We were all still laughing, clutching each other as we made our way through the gloom when I realized what Henry was doing. He was holding a miniature chalkboard and was scraping a nail down it. I shivered. Who's idea had that been?

A skeleton swooped down from the ceiling and more screams erupted. We walked a few more feet, everyone in our group and the one behind us torn between terror and hysterics, even though it wasn't all that scary. Tom was trying to act cool, but as soon as a fog machine blew a gust toward him he nearly jumped in Hamish's arms and we all laughed so hard we weren't breathing. The group behind us had to go ahead while we huddled off to the side, batting away spider webs and doubled over catching our breath.

By the time we made it to the kitchen door, all of us had spilled half our drinks. "We'd better get a mop before someone breaks their neck!" Lacuna whisper-shouted seriously when we realized this. But we all just fell into more fits of laughter.

I felt like a teenager again, when everything is doubly funny because you're with your friends. Our drink messes were abandoned (because *'how will we find them, anyway?'* Hamish wisely pointed out), and we busted through the door into the kitchen.

It was dark and dreary, but I could immediately tell Aramis was in there. Somewhere lurking. I could feel his eyes on me. It occurred to me then that Dreads have excellent night vision. I think I'd read that somewhere—

An arm wrapped around my waist and I screamed, all of my friends lurching toward me, shouting my name. Too fast for them to catch me, I was pulled behind a curtain of black gauze, the darkness thick, inky. Even when I was set on my feet and steadied, that arm still didn't leave my waist. And I knew that scent.

An orb of my magic popped up next to Aramis's face,

illuminating him in a tinge of glowing silver light, like a tiny moon. His bright green gaze moved from my eyes to my lips and back up.

"Is this part of the haunted tour?" I asked, a bit breathlessly.

"Only for you." His face lowered toward mine and I sucked in a small breath.

The lights flicked on, a jarring, horrible brightness. Aramis pulled back, blinking and confused. We couldn't see anyone else, but the din was loud—everyone was at a loss and bummed at the interruption to the spooky fun. Then, a blood-curdling scream broke through the haze.

Aramis and I locked eyes for a split second before we ran through the fog toward the scream, dodging all the gauze, spider webs, and decor that looked so paltry and crude in the light.

We found Maggie shaking, her hand covering her mouth as she pointed at a lump on the floor. Tom was leaning over next to Mags, looking like he might be sick. Hamish was pulling Maggie away, wrapping his arms around her. Lacuna had her phone out, shouting into it.

Aramis jumped into action. "Hamish, get Maggie water and get her outside." He looked at me and pointed to Tom. "Name?" I stammered his name and Aramis addressed him. "Tom, go get some air." Tom didn't react, so Aramis went over and helped him up. "Hey, buddy, go get some air, alright? Go with Hamish and Maggie. Everyone else," his voice rose with the command, "stay back, but do not leave." He turned to me again. "Are you okay?"

I was going to be sick, too. My Witchy sense was flooding in too quickly, making me nauseous. Dizzy and shaky. "Aramis, I think—"

"Everybody out!" a gruff, familiar voice barrelled through the café. "Outside! But do not leave under any circumstances!"

I heard his footsteps before I saw him. Sheriff Oliphant pushed aside a black cloth and stopped. He looked at me first and I felt an inch tall. Then his expression turned horribly sad just for a second before he looked at Aramis, seething.

"I suggest the two of you step away from that body."

Aramis grasped my hand and pulled me out of the café and into the cool night air. The minutes that passed by seemed like hours. Maggie was crying on Hamish's shoulder, Aramis was pacing, and Tom was huddled on the ground. I looked everywhere for Lacuna and found her talking with Deputy Pete. Apparently, she'd gotten a good look at the victim.

"It was Steven," Aramis said from behind me and I jumped.

Oh, Goddess. I sank onto the curb and Aramis sat next to me, his head in his hands. "I– His shirt. He insisted on wearing that shirt tonight. That's how I knew it was him."

When he said it, I realized I had taken in more information than I'd initially thought, just like last time. Steven had on a black shirt that said, *Eat, Drink, and Be Scary* in that greenish-yellow-tinted lettering that glows in the dark. The build and hair definitely fit Steven's description, too. The knife in his back was also a pretty good indication he hadn't seen the attack coming.

"Are you alright?" I asked stupidly, my hands shaking.

"No." Aramis's voice hardly carried and I reached out to clasp his arm.

The crowd began to part, everyone scuttling back like a predator had arrived. When I saw why, I knew one had.

"Aramis Hawthorne," Sheriff Oliphant said roughly, and Aramis stood. "You are under arrest for the murder of one John Doe." He pulled out handcuffs and I watched in horror as Aramis turned around without protest, his wrists together. "And you are now a suspect in the death of Steven Littlebottom."

CHAPTER 21

As soon as the strobe of red and blue police lights faded down the street, I launched into a run, shouting for Lacuna to follow me. Bless her soul, my friend didn't even bat an eye or ask what we were doing, she just ran alongside me.

I skidded to a stop in front of *Stonewood*, pathetically out of breath. "I need in."

Lacuna nodded once and pulled the key from her pocket. We dashed in, Hamish and Maggie hurrying in after us.

"Hamish," I commanded, rounding the corner of the counter. "Get Maggie home. Lac, check on Tom and then tell Mom and everyone what's happened." No one moved. "Go! Now!"

Like scurrying bugs, they all fled. I snatched up the broom Aunt Millie had given me and ran out into the street. The crowd was chaotic, news slowly spreading through the carnival that Gloam Hollow had seen another murder. I pushed against the throng, trying to find any clear patch of ground to launch from. I hadn't ridden a broom in so long, I wasn't sure how well I'd do taking off, but I had to try. It would be much faster than getting there on foot. We all know I'm not going to sprint.

After a couple of false starts, I managed to get the broom and myself up into the sky. I was wobbly at first but soon found my bearings. Like riding a bike. A few of the bats flying below the stars tittered at me, but my mind was far too distracted to translate.

There. The Sheriff's Department was just beyond those trees. I barely avoided a crash landing, but I'd made it. Oliphant's cruiser was out front, empty. I slammed my broom up against the side of it, hoping to dent the door or at least leave a scratch, but nothing happened. Fists clenched, I stormed into the office and right past Mrs. Cobblepot's empty desk. She was probably at the carnival along with everyone else.

"Corbin Oliphant!" I shouted, standing in the middle of the hallway.

The sheriff finished locking the door to the one holding cell in the place. He turned to me with a wan face and strode over before I could see Aramis in the cell. Taking my arm, not unkindly, he pulled me toward his office, but I yanked out of his grip just past Cobblepot's desk.

"You can't arrest someone without probable cause!"

I watched his jaw clench, but his blue eyes were sad. "I know what I need to arrest someone, Blair," he bit out, "and, unfortunately, I have it."

I shifted on my feet, pulse loud in my ears. "I don't believe you."

I'd never seen Corbin look so tired. Something about it made me want to cry. But I refused. Without a word, he lifted his arm and gestured toward his door. Feeling a thousand different things, I looked far down the hall toward the cell, then followed the sheriff into his cramped office.

Neither of us sat. Sheriff Oliphant pulled out a cardboard box labeled EVIDENCE, and I vaguely wondered if it was safe to leave that kind of thing out in the open. He removed the lid from the box and pulled out a plastic baggie, sliding it across the desk toward me.

I looked from it to him, incredulous. "A green hair? So, what? Hamish even had green hair today."

"Not just any green hair," he said quietly, taking the baggie back from me. "I found it in Art's the day we went in to look around."

Crossing my arms, I continued speaking disrespectfully. "Again, I say: *so, what*? There are several people in this town with green hair who could have gone in Art's for any number of reasons."

We hadn't even found evidence that the killer for sure went through Art's the night of the murder. Though, I guess Sheriff Oliphant thought he had.

"I just got the results back from a lab in the city not an hour ago. That's why I was headed to the café in the first place. The hair was confirmed to be a Dread Monster hair. A *male* Dread, which I don't think I have to remind you is very rare."

"He could have gone in Art's for candy. To say hello. To introduce himself. Besides, his hair is in dreadlocks and wrapped most of the time!" The last bit came out like a warbled, petulant shout.

Sheriff Oliphant's tired face turned red, angry. He reached into the EVIDENCE box and pulled something out, slamming it on the desk in front of me. The large plastic bag crinkled in his grip, sticky splotches of rusty brown clinging to the sides of it. "And this?" he ground out.

My vision was going a bit spotted, my pulse fully roaring in my ears. "It's a kitchen knife," I said, my voice weak, unconvincing. "Everyone has those."

"One that is the exact same brand as a knife that killed Steven Littlebottom in the café tonight?"

I blinked rapidly. That alarming fact had not escaped my notice. "Anyone could have that brand. We all buy kitchen knives." The logic was getting weaker and weaker along with my knees.

"Blair, this company only sells to licensed chefs. I looked them up when we found this knife in the trash outside the bakery."

"C—Cory, the inn's cook— He took culinary classes, maybe he—" But Cory had surely been off with Betty tonight, celebrating their engagement.

Oliphant's demeanor had shifted from anger to pity. It was so much worse. "Cory took a couple of cooking classes at the local college. He is not licensed by a fancy school like Aramis Hawthorne."

I dropped into a chair. I didn't even know Aramis had gone to culinary school.

Corbin sat down next to me and took my hand. "What do you really know about this guy, darlin'?"

Nothing. Enough. "I have to go," I choked out.

Sheriff called after me, but I was out the door and back on my broom in a flash. I soared up and over the department, landing in the trees next to it. Crouched down, I hid behind a bush, watching the front entrance. Corbin came out after me but assumed I was already gone. He shook his head and rubbed at his tired eyes before going back in.

I didn't have my spelled notebook and pen, so I made owl calls until one swooped down and landed in the branches above me. Carefully, I asked the Great Horned Owl to deliver a message to Mom at the inn. While I awaited her response, I sent a hastily crafted spell toward a window. The Sheriff Department's wards had Great-Grandma Wardwell's signature on them, and I prayed that magic would respond to me, regardless of Oliphant's.

Several long moments of torturous silence later, the owl swooped back down and landed in front of me with a note attached to his leg.

You better know what you're doing, Pumpkin

A second later, I heard the faint trill of a cell phone ringing inside the office. I watched through the glowing window as Sheriff Oliphant answered it curtly. A look of alarm passed over him and I read his lips say the name, "Minnie," before he slammed the phone down and ran out of the department, throwing a spell over his shoulder at the locks. His cruiser squealed away and I spelled open the window.

Aramis

I'd been in the cell for all of half a second before I heard Wardwell shout from the hallway.

Isn't it the man who's supposed to be running after the

girl to save her? Huffing a laugh, I shook my head, listening to her berate poor Oliphant. That Witch has me by the throat and it could be a huge problem.

Their voices faded away and I assumed he'd taken her somewhere to show her the knife missing from my kitchen and the hair he'd found.

If I wasn't the one in it, I would have laughed at this holding cell. It looks like a little old lady's room in an assisted living center. There was even a lamp with a fringed lampshade. I pulled the thin chain to turn it on and studied it for a second. Surely they wouldn't be stupid enough to leave anything in this cell. I checked it—bolted down. Alright, they weren't *that* stupid, then.

I sat hard on the small bed smashed up against one wall and the bars, made up with a crocheted quilt. Eventually, Oliphant would stomp in here and give me one phone call. But I couldn't make the one necessary, not from here. I should've made it days ago. I'd let Blair and this damned Harvest Festival distract me.

Blair

He had his head in his hands, sitting in that ridiculous cell that looked like it belonged in a nursing home. My boots scuffed on the floor and he looked up.

"Hey, Wardwell." Aramis stood, fisting the bars.

"Murder, huh?" Adrenaline was still pumping thick in my veins, and I couldn't control my irritated, scared tone.

He tried to smile, but it fell flat. The lines around his eyes were deeper. Like he was scared, too, and trying to convince himself he wasn't. "I know everyone says it, but I didn't do this."

Goddess, I want to believe him. "Then you'd better help me prove that." I looked nervously back toward the door. "And quickly. He's going to be back any minute."

Aramis scooted up closer to the bars. The cell was so small, he barely fit between the bed and the table. Part of a hand-crocheted blanket drooped out between the bars to touch my knees. "Wardwell, I don't think–"

"If you want my help, you need to start talking. Now." There was only cold calculation in my voice and I'd take that over the fear any day.

After a moment of searching my face, his throat bobbed and he spoke. "Listen very carefully." The intensity in his eyes made my heart slam against my breastbone—if it had ever stopped doing so since the murder. "Look up a man named Reginald Davies in Longbrook, New Haven. It will be listed with RapidTitle Loans, LLC."

I blinked. None of what he said was making sense. He must have picked up on my trepidation because he reached through the bars and clasped my hand.

"You don't have to do this. You can walk away right now. I won't tell anyone you were here."

My Witch sense tingled. Even if it hadn't, I could see the sincerity in him, almost like a glow. I rarely see auras as clearly as Aunt Millie does, but I could see Aramis's now, and it was white with ribbons of gold and orchid woven through it. Purity, altruism, and idealism. But the longer I looked at him, the more grayish-yellow it was turning. He was truly scared.

I squeezed his hand and put my other palm to his cheek,

just for a second. "Reginald Davies in Longbrook, New Haven. RapidTitle Loans. What else?"

The breath of relief he let out was audible. "When he answers, you'll need to say these exact words: Hi, Reg, this is Kenny's sister, Julia. I have one of those bikes you were looking for in the East Village."

I was taking furious mental notes, cursing myself for not adding actual detective props to my costume, like a *notebook.*

"He will ask you if the bike is purple or green and you have to tell him green."

"Because of your hair?" I asked without thinking that perhaps it was a ridiculous leap to make. But he smiled at me and my stomach flipped, thinking stupidly of that almost-kiss in the café.

Did I almost kiss a murderer? Let one carry me upstairs and tuck me in bed? I shivered and pushed those thoughts away. I could't think like that.

"Yes, because of my hair. He will ask you if the bike is in good condition and you'll say yes."

"Because you're safe?"

He fingered my silly detective hat through the bars. "Because he needs to know I'm still here in Gloam Hollow where he left me."

My curiosity got the better of me. "And if you weren't?"

That smirk I'd grown to adore lifted one side of his mouth. "You would say, 'Fair condition. It runs.'" I had so many questions, but Aramis kept going. "When he comes, you might recognize him. I'll tell you everything once he gets here. This is far bigger than me."

I heard the crunch of gravel beneath tires outside, coming from the front of the department. Quick as lightning, I squeezed Aramis's hand and dropped it, running for the window I'd snuck in through. I barely made it out and got it closed before Deputy Pete went in the front. I watched him for a moment from my hiding place outside. He sat hard in a chair and took off his cowboy hat, his head hanging. The most trouble Pete had ever seen before the last couple of weeks was probably the fight he once had to break up between two teenagers who were seeing the same girl. Poor guy didn't sign up for this in a sleepy town like Gloam Hollow.

I took a few steadying breaths, then went for my broom hidden in the trees. Hand wrapped around the handle, I realized I didn't know where to go. I didn't have time to field questions from the family or my friends. Someone killed Steven and the Golem John Doe. The longer Aramis was in jail for it, the longer the real murderer walked free. Sheriff Oliphant would likely be with Steven's body at the morgue by now if Mom hadn't held him up too much with her decoy. Maggie and Hamish would be at the cottage, Mom and Grandma and who knows who else at the inn.

I growled in frustration. Maybe I did need one of those Goddess-awful cell phones.

I hopped onto the broom and flew to Wardwell Cottage, sending up pleas that no one would deter me. Hamish was probably my best bet. Here's hoping I could avoid Mags for a bit, though I felt awful for thinking it. She'd been the one to find poor Steven.

I found Hamish sitting on the edge of Maggie's bed. He caught my eye and his widened, but I held a finger to my lips and gestured toward our sleeping cousin. Hamish adjusted her blankets and then tip-toed out into the hallway.

He barely had the door shut before he was whisper-shouting at me.

"*What* were you thinking? Where did you go? Are you crazy?"

"Are you going to let me answer any of those questions or keep berating me?" I crossed my arms and Hamish huffed. Still, he followed me up to his room, where I sat at his desk and opened the laptop.

"What are you doing? Slow down, B, please." The pleading in his voice made me go still.

"Aramis didn't do this," I said, testing the words out on my tongue. My Witchy sense had never lied to me before but there was a very real chance I was blinded by my growing feelings for Aramis.

"Blair..."

"Just listen. I don't believe he did this, even if the evidence is stacked against him." By the time I finished telling Hamish what that evidence was, he was looking a bit green. "He told me to contact a man and tell him some very specific things, I assume some sort of code between them."

I turned back to the laptop, attempting to figure out how to turn the thing on, but Hamish slammed it shut. "You realize what a terrible idea this is, right? What if you contact this guy and your code is telling him to come here and eliminate all witnesses or something and break Aramis out of jail?"

I couldn't say the thought hadn't occurred to me. "I know, but I have a plan." If I got to the point in the conversation with this *Reginald* guy where I was to reveal Aramis was still in Gloam Hollow, but it didn't feel right, I would redirect him. Tell him the *bike* was 'running.'

"This is the worst idea you've ever had," Hamish complained, "and you've had some pretty terrible ones."

"Shut up and show me how to use this thing," I hissed, opening the laptop again.

It took about five seconds for Hamish to pull up several Reginald Davies in Longbrook, but only one number matched the number of Longbrook RapidTitle Loans. Hamish handed me his cell phone and I dialed with shaking hands. We stared at each other wide-eyed as it rang on speakerphone, I think as a means to ground ourselves. After three rings there was a little click.

"RapidTitle, this is Reg," a gruff voice came over the line.

My eyes bulged at Hamish and he pushed my leg, mouthing at me to *talk*. "Hi, Reg, this is Kenny's sister, Julia."

Silence. "Julia?" the voice asked. "Haven't heard from you in a while. How ya' been?"

Oh, Goddess. This wasn't in the plan. And if anyone was listening in on this conversation, it was pretty obvious Reg didn't like this *Julia* very much.

"Ah, good. Good," the words tumbled out. Hamish motioned erratically for me to talk.

"Good to hear. How's that cat of yours? Puck, isn't it?"

I thought Hamish was going to pass out. Was this man testing me? How did he know about my cat? I pressed one thumb into the center of my palm to balance myself. Where was a nice bag of crystals when a Witch needed it?

"Puck is good," I said, proud of how smooth my voice sounded. "How's your mom?" I don't even know where the words came from or what possessed me to ask such a thing. Hamish smacked my knee and we traded various aggressive hand gestures in the silent family code of: *shut up, stop it, what are you doing?*

The voice, *Reg*, gave a deep chuckle. "She's good. Ornery as ever."

Had I just chosen the right thing to say or was this a game for whomever might be listening in? Did this guy and Aramis have *bugged* phone conversations?

"What can I do for ya', Jules?" Reg sounded amiable, but I could sense a note of concern in his tone. Worry, even.

I went through the conversation as Aramis had scripted it and by the time Reginald said, "I'll come by in the morning to check it out," the tension underneath his voice was thick.

He hung up and Hamish and I just stared at each other for a moment.

"What do we do now?" he finally asked.

"We wait."

CHAPTER 22

Aramis

S itting in this granny cell all night, I hadn't slept a wink. Instead, I'd nursed a boiling rage until I couldn't see straight. All it did was amp up the feeling of being a caged animal, so I eventually sat on the rickety bed and rattled off the titles of every song on every album I had up in my apartment. The only personal effects from my old life I'd brought with me to Gloam Hollow.

I heard the front door of the Sheriff's Office open. Slow steps and humming—Mrs. Cobblepot. I watched as best I could through the bars and down the hall as she shuffled to her desk to set her purse down. She clicked the button on an old-style answering machine and sorted through the mail while she listened to three messages about petty grievances and one of someone claiming they had evidence regarding the coffee shop boy's attack.

Mrs. Cobblepot jotted notes, then stood and shuffled her

way down to my cell. "Hello, dear. Criminals need breakfast as well, don't you think? Would you rather have biscuits and gravy or a quiche?"

Whoever put this frail woman in charge of a Sherrif's Office needed their head examined. Unless... I looked more closely at her, at the little flinty glint in her eyes... I couldn't believe it. I schooled my features so I wouldn't show the shock. Did this town have any idea their darling Mrs. Cobblepot was a Dragonborn? An extremely rare form of Dragon that is less beast and more mortal, but they can certainly shift into ferocious fire-breathers when provoked.

"I'm not hungry, Mrs. Cobblepot, thank you," I finally said before my inspection of her could become obvious. "I would gladly take coffee or tea if you have it, though."

"You're such a polite young man." She looked at me with genuine pity. "And all the help you've given this community in such a short time?" She *tisked*. "Shame. Certainly, I'll bring you a pot of coffee, dear."

True to her word, Mrs. Cobblepot brought me an entire carafe of coffee, as well as one of orange juice and a box of Minerva Wardwell's donuts *'in case I changed my mind.'* If I hadn't just realized she was a Dragon, I would have thought she was insane to give a prisoner anything that could be used as a weapon. But, I was pretty sure no one would make it out of the Sheriff's Department that Mrs. Cobblepot didn't allow to.

I looked down at the donut box, *Toil & Truffle* stamped on the front. These, however, were the real fright. I'd done my research since meeting Blair and I knew just how powerful the Wardwell Witches were. I'd also learned Minerva was as likely to spell these to break me out as she was to spell them to poison me. I had no intention of escaping or vomiting up my guts, but I was still very curious.

Slowly, I opened the lid. Just donuts. Regular old donuts.

But then the sprinkles started sliding and scooting across the bottom of the box, coalescing into a message.

Reg coming -W

Wardwell.

I had what was probably a very doofy grin on my face when Sheriff Oliphant walked up, his keys and cuffs jingling. I coughed into the box, dispersing the sprinkles and hopefully deterring anyone else from trying to eat one of the donuts.

"Sheriff," I said, standing and setting the box aside.

Oliphant sighed heavily, then raised his voice over his shoulder, echoing down the hall, "Ethel, how many times have I said you can't feed people in the holding cell?"

"You can't torture prisoners, Corbin," Mrs. Cobblepot shouted back.

When he turned back to me, he looked grim. "I'm going to take you into a room where we can sit down and talk."

Oh, great. I was going to get Nice Cop. I fought the urge to roll my eyes. I already knew every trick this pony had. One look at the evidence I already knew was in his possession and I could pick up on everything he'd missed. I just needed one look.

"*Talk*, huh?" I said snarkily, not helping matters.

He unlocked the cell door and cuffed me. Though I thought of seven different ways to disarm the man and considered the three different chances I had to let one of my vipers slither loose, I was perfectly reasonable and followed Oliphant to a small room. We sat across from one another at a table and stared.

Blair

"Peanuts on a window sill!" I cursed, clutching my chest. I had to assume the giant man who stepped out from behind a tree next to Wardwell Cottage was Reginald because he did look vaguely familiar. But that realization came *after* my mind whirred with the possibility I was being ambushed by a murderer.

"Sorry, Blair," he said. "Didn't mean to startle you." His tone was still gruff like it had been on the phone and everything about him screamed motorcycle gang, but there was something kind in his eyes.

"You're Reginald?" I stepped off the last step of the porch and strode forward, but I kept magic at the ready—just in case. No sense in being an idiot.

"Name's Kenny, actually." He held out his hand and I shook it. "I'll need to debrief with you later, but right now I need you to tell me where Aramis is."

Debrief? Was Kenny a cop? "He's being held at the Sheriff's Department, under arrest for one count of murder and he's a suspect in another."

Kenny let loose a string of words that Grandma Wardwell would swat him for saying in front of a lady. "Look," he said in a low voice when he was done cursing, "you need to watch yourself, okay? Aramis did not do this, I can promise you that. And until we figure out who did, you aren't safe."

He turned toward his motorcycle which had been hidden in the foggy shadows of the trees, but I rushed to catch up. "Wait. I want to go with you."

"No." Without another word or even a backward glance, Kenny hopped on his bike, started it up, and sped off down the road.

There's one more thing you should know about Wardwells. We hate being told *no*.

Griping and grousing, I stomped to the porch and retrieved my broom.

I beat him to the Sheriff's Office by three seconds. I stood on the landing blocking the door, and Kenny stared me down with his jaw tight. I crossed my arms and lifted my chin.

"*No wonder*," he muttered under his breath. Whatever that meant. He bent at the waist and stuck a finger in my face. "Stay *out* of the way, and stay silent."

I cast a concealment spell and disappeared from in front of him. "That'll work," he said through gritted teeth, and I hoped he was right.

Kenny charged through the door, crashing in like he owned the place. "Where is Aramis Hawthorne?" he bellowed, and I followed him.

Mrs. Cobblepot, unbothered by a giant, unfamiliar man barrelling into her workplace, stood slowly. "And you are?"

"Robert Carlisle," he rattled off. "I'm his attorney."

I was glad I was invisible because my face instantly screwed up in confusion. Reginald, Kenny, Robert... Who was this guy?

Sheriff Oliphant came around the corner then, steam just about coming out of his ears and I squeezed my eyes shut. Our Wardwell magic is stronger than Oliphant's, but there was a fifty-fifty chance he could see through my concealment spell.

"I want to see my client now," Kenny (Robert?) demanded of the sheriff with a growl.

Corbin looked only at the intruder, not even a flicker of attention in my direction, and I let out a breath. "You're his attorney?" Oliphant asked, his tone clipped, patience worn very thin. "I thought you were a construction worker brought in for the café."

This got more confusing by the minute. "I don't care what you thought, you backwater cop. Now show me to my client."

I thought Corbin might snarl at the guy, but he showed him down the hall to a small room. And then I thought Kenny would rip off Corbin's arms.

"An interrogation room? You will not speak to my client without me present. Do you understand?" Kenny thundered.

Sheriff Oliphant let him in and closed the automatic-lock door, with me on the wrong side of it.

I sat on the floor outside the room for what felt like hours, listening to Mrs. Cobblepot hum and the thrum of Kenny and Aramis's voices in the room behind me. My cloaking spell would only hold for so long before I became too exhausted.

I was falling asleep, my head against the wall when the door opened. Kenny had one foot out the door when I heard Aramis say, "Send her in, Ken. Please."

Kenny sighed and held the door open with his foot, looking around. "You out here, Blair?" he whispered.

I tapped his arm and he flinched, snarling. "Hurry up and don't get caught."

I slipped past him, the door closing and locking automatically behind me.

Letting the spell drop, I watched as Aramis's eyes focused on me. "We don't have much time," he said, his voice raspy, like he'd been talking too much and hadn't gotten any sleep.

I sat across from him, turning to look at the door every few seconds. "I think you have a lot to explain to me," I said.

"I do. I'm going to try and make it as fast and concise as possible." It was easy to see the trepidation on him, in the lines of his face and the downturn of his lips. "I came here to leave my old life behind. Gloam Hollow was supposed to be a fresh start for me. I—" His words broke off and he sat back in his chair, running a hand along his jaw, his wrists bound and the cuffs rattling. "I was a police officer for a long time, then, I became a detective."

I tried to control my shock and let him finish.

"There were so many dirty cops, I couldn't take it. I ended up with too many enemies and eventually left the force altogether to be a Private Investigator. I would collect intel for my clients, and work with the good detectives like Kenny in my old precinct to bring down the bad guys."

I felt absolutely terrible for ever doubting him. I wanted to say so, but he kept going, the words tumbling out faster and faster, probably worried we'd be out of time soon.

"I made even more enemies through my P.I. work. Eventually, I had to leave the city. Kenny is an old buddy of mine through the force and then P.I. and undercover work, too. He's essentially become my handler."

"And your attorney?" I asked, irritated I'd chosen that as my first question.

Aramis half-heartedly chuckled. "That, too. We know a lot of people in the tech world and black markets... Kenny erased me, and I moved here."

"Sheriff Oliphant said you are a licensed chef. That's how he connected you to all this. The knives are only sold to licensed chefs."

Aramis tapped his thumbs together repeatedly. "That was forged. Although, I'll hand it to the sheriff for connecting the dots."

"And the blood outside the café?" I could hear the strain in my voice and hoped Aramis couldn't.

The corners of his lips turned down. "One of my guys cut himself moving in the oven. That blood wasn't even there until after I was questioned by Oliphant the first time."

I wanted to sit down. Relief was pulsing through me as much as adrenaline and it was a dizzying combination. "So someone is framing you? Stole your knives from the cafè and set you up?"

Aramis nodded. "That's what we think, yeah."

I stood, almost toppling my chair. "You have to tell Sheriff Oliphant. It's all a mistake, and he can let you out and—"

"Wardwell, Wardwell," he interrupted me. "Slow down. It's safer for everyone if I'm in here. We have a plan, but right now you need to leave before Oliphant sees you. Go find Kenny."

More than a little off-kilter, I cloaked myself in magic and left the interrogation room. Kenny was berating poor Corbin for all of his shortcomings on what I assumed was a fabricated list designed to keep him occupied while I'd talked to Aramis. Thank the Goddess the sheriff had his back to me because concealment spells rarely worked where he was concerned.

Careful not to startle Kenny or accidentally alert Corbin, I picked up a piece of paper and waved it lightly. Kenny abruptly finished his sentence and shouted, "Good day!" to the sheriff and Mrs. Cobblepot before storming out.

Once he was on his motorcycle, I kicked a rock to show him I was there. He'd already put on his helmet, so his voice was muffled, but he commanded, "Meet me at the café."

I couldn't hold the cloaking spell any longer, so I ran to the woods and let it fall. Hopefully, I had enough strength to fly my broom to the square at least.

If someone had framed Aramis, wouldn't they be watching the café? Wasn't it a crime scene still? Thinking along this line for the entire ride, I elected to use the last of my energy to cloak myself and touch down behind the shops. Apparently, I had the right idea, because that's where Kenny's motorcycle was parked. He hopped off, unhooking a black toolbox from his bike. Whistling, he approached the back door and unlocked it—just a construction worker back to check a few things.

Thank Goddess for small-town police forces, because no one was patrolling the interior. Except Henry. I shut and bolted the back door, letting my spell fall. I was *exhausted*.

"We'll go up to the apartment," Kenny said.

"Do you hear that?" I whispered, and Kenny looked around, listening.

"I don't hear anything."

"Oh, no." I rushed through the back and into the kitchen, swatting haunted house decorations out of my way. "Henry." I knelt before the ghost where he sat on the floor crying.

"Hi Ken," Henry said through his tears, looking behind me. "Hey, Blair."

Kenny did not respond, so I assumed he couldn't see my specter friend. "Henry says hello."

"Oh, hey, buddy. This has to be tough on you."

It was clear Aramis trusted Kenny, but I'd been on the fence about being alone with a strange man until he spoke so kindly and sincerely to Henry.

I translated for the two of them for a bit, and Henry's invisible tears finally dried up. It seemed that Henry, Aramis, and Kenny had spent quite a lot of time together during the weeks of preparing for the café to open. Now we all worried it would never happen. Henry had also grown close to Steven since he was hired.

This death would not be an easy one for our little town to get over.

When Henry was consoled, Kenny and I went upstairs to Aramis's apartment.

"What are we doing up here?" I asked as we climbed the stairs, unsure what to make of it all.

"Aramis has what we call a 'Go Bag' hidden under the floorboards. It has all the information necessary to prove who he was before Gloam Hollow. I'm going to take the bag and you're going to go back to your cottage and ensure you aren't alone, *ever*, for the next few days."

I halted, trying to formulate a nice way of saying: '*um you have zero say over me*,' but the giant man sighed, turning around to face me on the stairs.

"No one is holding you hostage. Whoever framed Aramis has been watching. And if anyone has watched him for two seconds in this town, they would know you're the easiest way to make him do what they want. He asked me to make sure you'd be safe."

I didn't know if I should be flattered or terrified. "Why would someone do this to Aramis?" I asked as we climbed the rest of the way up and Kenny unlocked the door.

"Aramis was one hell of a cop and an even better detective. But that means he's made a lot of enemies, and some of them are powerful. We know who many of them are and we'll start there."

I tried not to enter more than about a foot inside the door. The entire apartment smelled of Aramis and looked like him with dark walls and rustic furniture. One entire wall was just floor-to-ceiling shelves of vinyl records, a smaller shelf of books across the room from it. I didn't want to see any more, not without him present. It felt like a violation, a jump in our new friendship.

Kenny stomped around the place, doing heel-toe taps until he found the right board and pried it up. He reached in, down almost to his shoulder, and yanked up a small duffle bag. With a quick unzip, he ruffled around in it and zipped it back up, setting the board back in its place. "That'll do it. Now let's get you home."

Kenny drove me on his motorcycle, then walked me all the way to the front porch. It felt like one of those dates you go on and he walks you to the door but you didn't hit it off as more than friends, and you can't wait for him to leave. Only in this case, it seemed Kenny felt the same about me. "Thanks," I said dumbly.

"You should know that I'd do anything for Aramis. He's the brother I chose and I won't stop until the real killer is found."

Alright, so I did like Kenny in some regard. He turned to leave, and I trudged to the door feeling like I was wading through gelatin, but I had a ridiculous question eating at me. My face screwed up, I turned around. "Wait. Why *Julia*? Who's Julia?"

Kenny took a long moment to answer, his face stone-cold, but I could tell he was contemplating whether to answer me or not. "Before I left him here, Aramis insisted you needed a code name. He said you were already important to him, but he wasn't yet sure why." He looked at me intensely. "I take it you both know now?"

CHAPTER 23

The cottage was packed full of Wardwells.

And everyone was talking at once.

Evidently, Aramis had sent Kenny to my grandmother's inn last night, and everyone had done this fun little thing this morning where they began making a schedule of who would babysit me when. They were still sitting all around the kitchen discussing it like I was a child. I debated screaming that I could take care of myself, but I did not. What I did do was much worse.

I used my new favorite cloaking spell and left the cottage.

Kenny might be good at what he does and Aramis might be an excellent detective, but I could help. I've never been one to sit on the sidelines in a corner when something needs to be done. Being a damsel in distress wasn't in my wheelhouse and it wasn't going to start now.

Once I was far enough down the tree tunnel road, I dropped the spell and sifted through what I knew.

Sheriff Oliphant had two knives from the café in

evidence as murder weapons, and a strand of green hair confirmed to be that of a male Dread Monster. It would have been easy for any of the construction guys to steal the knives. It wouldn't have been that difficult to get one of Aramis's hairs, either. He kept the hair wrap on all the time that I'd seen him, but it wasn't impossible. He had to take it off *sometimes*. Like in the shower. (I blushed.) Or when he changes shirts or sleeps.

I decided to veer off toward the library. Maybe I could find books on Golems to learn more about the first victim. I couldn't see a connection with Steven, but I had to begin somewhere.

My first stop in the library, however, was the ancient coffee machine free to the public. It was either going to be light brown bean water or sludgy tar. Alas, I couldn't let anyone know where I was, and that meant my coffee options were limited. The cups were flimsy, too, and I frowned. Surely I could be less of a coffee snob for one day. Just one. Then, maybe tomorrow I could use all the pretty mugs and drink all the best coffee.

"Let's see," I said to myself as I put the paper cup under the spout and pressed. Option number two: sludge. Well, that was better than weak bean water. I think.

The first two sips were utterly intolerable. After that, the caffeine addiction kicked in and a fix was a fix.

I set up shop at a table in a far back corner, in case Hamish came into work today. I didn't want him to catch me. Then, I wandered around the stacks finding every book I could on Golems and even a couple on Dread Monsters. Once I had a towering stack, I sat at my table and took pages and pages of notes. Hours later, nothing had connected, but it felt like I was headed in the right direction at least.

Then Hamish found me.

"Do you want to send me to an early grave?" he spat. "Or what about your mother? She's been worried sick. You just vanished!"

"How is Maggie?"

"Distraught. She found a dead body, B, and you've just been M.I.A!"

"I'm sorry." I folded my arms and slammed my head down on them on the desk. "This isn't right." My voice was muffled and Hamish yanked me upright. "They have the wrong guy, and that means the correct guy is still out there somewhere. We need to find him."

"Or her. Don't be sexist."

I snorted and Hamish gave me a small grin. "Or her," I amended.

Hamish sat unceremoniously. "What do you have so far?"

I filled him in on all the details he didn't already know, and together we combed through information about Golems.

"So," Hamish read off our list, "they can appear like anyone they've been in contact with, but only for a short period of time. They tend to live in colonies, sticking together. They have almost cult-like tendencies and often have a particular symbol for their clan."

Could that be why the murdered Golem had a bird tattoo? Was that some symbol of his clan? It would certainly narrow things down for us. But what was he doing in town? And what had he done that ended in his murder in a place like Gloam Hollow?

I massaged my temples and Hamish tapped a pencil to his chin.

"I'm hungry," I griped, grabbing my bag to rummage around in it for any forgotten snack that might be at the bottom.

"I have a sandwich in the break room fridge." Hamish shrugged.

"Pass." I pulled out the piece of stick candy Art had given me the other day in his shop. Better than nothing, even though I had to pull some fuzz off of it. I ripped open the package and twirled it between my teeth as we worked.

Hamish sniffed after a few minutes, getting close to my mouth. "What flavor is that?"

I pushed him back. "Get off me. It's watermelon."

"Huh," he said, turning back to the book in front of him. "I'm surprised you didn't get tutti frutti. That was always your favorite when we were kids."

Every hair on the back of my neck stood on end and I froze, the candy hanging half out of my mouth. "Hamish," I whispered, yanking out the sugar stick. "Hamish..."

"What?" He watched my slow, sloth-like panicked realization. "Oh my, Goddess. You figured something out, didn't you?"

"We need to call Sheriff Oliphant, now!"

Hamish fished in his pocket and pulled out his cell phone. I quickly dialed the number and Sheriff Oliphant answered on the first ring. "Hamish! Have you found her?"

"It's me," I said, my throat feeling suddenly thick for how worried he was about me.

"Oh thank goodness." His breath whooshed through the line. "Where are you? We've been so worried."

"I'm okay, I'm with Hamish at the library." Hamish gave me a warning glare and I realized my error. He would soon be in for an earful for not disclosing when and where he'd found me. That would have to wait. "Did Art ever tell you the name of the fishing hole he used to visit with your dad?"

Sheriff Oliphant was quiet for a moment, then slowly answered, "No, he didn't. Why are you asking me this?"

"Is that something Art would forget?"

Another pause. Then a begrudging, "No, it isn't. What's going on, Blair?"

"I have a hunch. I need you to look into it. Art offered me a piece of candy when we were there, remember?"

Oliphant made a sound of acknowledgment.

"He said to take watermelon because it was my favorite flavor when I was a kid. It seemed a little off when he said it, but I couldn't pinpoint why because I did always go straight for the stick candies when I was a Witchling. But Hamish just reminded me it was *tutti frutti* that was my go-to."

"Anyone can forget a customer's favorite flavor generations later, Blair. You forgot it yourself."

"Yes, but there was something strange about him that day, you have to admit it. Wasn't he your dad's best friend? Why would he forget their favorite place to go?"

There was a huff on the other end of the phone. "I did think he was odd that day, I'll admit. And I asked him about the fishing hole for that very reason, but Blair, Art is very old."

"Please just look into it. Go talk to Art, and do some digging. Something doesn't feel right."

Sheriff sighed, but he asked something that surprised me. "Do you know anything about this attorney of Hawthorne's?"

"I just know that you should trust him. And look somewhere else besides Aramis." I hung up before Corbin could prod any further or tell me no.

"You think something is up with Art?" Hamish asked, surprised. "He couldn't stab someone. He's so tiny and frail."

I flipped furiously through the book pages in front of us, looking for a random tidbit of information I'd seen that seemed useless at the time. When I found it I shouted, "Bingpot!" and Hamish hushed me. I pointed at the passage repeatedly until he read it.

"Golems and their closely related cousins, Mimics, have a strong taste for sugar. You will often find them drawn to places like ice cream and sweets shops," Hamish read aloud before turning to me with wide eyes. "You think—"

"I think Art isn't Art. I think he's a Golem. Maybe from the same clan as the one who was murdered."

I snatched Hamish's phone and dialed Sheriff Oliphant again. "A bird!" I said as soon as the phone stopped ringing. "Corbin, I think Art's been replaced with a Golem. And they stay in pairs or packs. They usually have some sort of mascot or symbol. The Golem victim had a sparrow tattoo on his wrist. Look for a bird tattoo or symbol."

"I'm headed to Art's shop now, but I have my doubts. How did the Golem manage to get through the spelled locks, hm?"

If he wanted to be sassy with me, I'd be sassy right back. "Well, how did you think Aramis did it, huh?"

"Oh my Goddess," Hamish whispered next to me, scrambling through the mess of open pages on the table.

I hung up before Sheriff Oliphant could finish whatever it was he was saying. "What?"

But Hamish had his nose buried in one of the books. When he turned to me, all the color had drained from his face and he was wearing a triumphant grin.

"What is it?" I breathed.

"Mimics can not only mimic a person's appearance like Golems can, but their magic, too."

"Like mimicking the magic of Lilly Tuttle to figure out how to get through Art's spelled locks!"

"Bingpot."

"Come on, Hamish. If that isn't Art, then we need to figure out where the real Art is."

CHAPTER 24

We rushed down the sidewalk of the square, avoiding the Harvest Festival patrons who had stuck around after the murder. Not even half of them had stayed, but I was thankful some had as we dodged anyone we might know.

"Do you know where Art lives?" I asked Hamish as it occurred to me that I did not.

"He owns that gray house kind of behind the bakery and the florist."

I almost tripped. I didn't, but I did pull at the sleeve of Hamish's tweed jacket. "Next to the yellow one?"

"Yep, that's the one."

Now things were beginning to make sense. "We need to get off the square before someone intercepts us."

"Here." Hamish grabbed my wrist and pulled me down a small alley between two shops. "Left on Pecan," he said.

Sure enough, it landed us just behind the shops and on Pecan Street which doubled as an alleyway. A couple blocks down sat the yellow house whose private trail led directly to

Dew Park, where Anon was attacked. On the other side of that trail was a small copse of trees, and a little gray house tucked up behind them. Just a hop and a skip from Art's *Candy Shop, Spectre, The Copper Cauldron*, and *Toil & Truffle*.

We rushed up the sidewalk and onto the porch. I banged the knocker, but no one answered. Hamish kept trying it, but I was getting antsy. My Witch sense was more than its usual tingling, it was like bursts of lightning all over and something felt very wrong.

"I'm going in," I finally told Hamish.

"How? His house will be spelled only for him, won't it?" The Wardwells and Tuttles try to spell even home locks with magic, but we can't possibly get to them all.

"Maybe, but if a Mimic did something to him, they had to get in somehow, right? They had to Mimic a Tuttle or Wardwell's magic."

There was a ward on his house, I could feel it. I sent out a tendril of magic to feel for a signature. A Tuttle spell. But there was a hole in it that had to be the work of a Mimic breaking down the spell. It felt very similar to the warped Tuttle magic on Art's locks at the shop.

My magic located the hole in the ward and I slipped through. Once I got past it, all I had to do was open the front door.

Hamish and I were in.

It was nothing special to the casual observer, an old home that had certainly seen many memories, but it was cozy and well-loved.

Walking on our toes through the living area, we heard a thud and traded alarmed looks. Then it came again, and again. Slowly, we made our way toward the sound. It was coming from the pantry in the kitchen. Nodding to one another, we both lifted one hand filled with magic ready to throw and together we flung open the pantry door.

Art fell out onto our feet, tied, gagged, and so pale. The *real* Art.

Hamish dialed the sheriff and paramedics while I untied Art and got him a glass of water.

"What happened, Art?" I prodded, trying to soothe him, but also pull as much information as possible from him in case he lost consciousness.

"It was days ago," he said, his voice weak and hands shaking as he tried to get the water glass to his lips. "A man walked into the shop." He shook his head. "I'd never seen him before, but he kept asking me peculiar questions about the building the new café is in. If I knew anything about the owner and if I'd met him. He eventually left, but a few nights later another strange fellow showed up here at my house. He knocked me over the head and I'd swear he looked like me all of a sudden. Then he tied me up and put me in the pantry."

It smelled absolutely atrocious in the pantry and I didn't want to embarrass Art by asking how he'd managed certain portions of life while he was trapped in there. "Did he feed you?" I asked.

He nodded. "Bread and a little water. But I've only seen his face twice since then. Once he still looked like me, but the next time he looked different."

"Like someone we know?"

"No, no. Just a regular Joe again."

"Tell me about him. Did he have anything distinguishing about him?" I was trying to follow his timeline, to see if the man was our John Doe lying in the morgue, or the Mimic that Oliphant and I had seen in Art's shop.

Art thought for a moment, water sloshing over the side of his cup as he trembled. "He had a little bird tattoo." He pointed at the inside of his bicep. "A sparrow, 'bout right there."

Bingpot. The dead Golem had a sparrow on his wrist.

"Do you remember when this was?" I prodded.

"No, honey, I don't." He rubbed at the back of his head and I heard sirens blaring.

"Were you at the town meeting about the Harvest Festival? When you said someone broke into your shop."

Art looked confused. "Yes, I remember that. That was the day after the first strange man came into my shop questioning me about the café owner. The other showed up at my house the day after all that rain started."

"And you're sure it was different men both times, not the same man with different faces?"

Art thought hard. "Well, honey, I guess I don't know... Do you mean a Golem?" He blinked a few times, surprise lifting his brows. "Haven't heard of a Golem in these parts in ages..."

Deputy Pete came running in then, Carla the paramedic close on his heels, so my questioning was halted. They ensured Art was stable and put him in an ambulance to be taken to the hospital for observation.

Hamish and I left the house and walked across to the apothecary. Shaken, I poured us both two fingers of whiskey. Hamish laughed, but there was no humor in it. "Is it even midday yet?"

"Sure it is, somewhere." We both downed the drink.

A few minutes later, Hamish's phone rang. "Sheriff," he told me, passing me the phone.

"Corbin!" I exclaimed frantically, clutching the phone to my ear.

"You were right, kid. That wasn't Art. Golems don't like being prodded, so I peppered him with useless questions until his glamor started to warble. I got a nice big glimpse of not only a different person under there but a bird tattoo on his bicep—a sparrow. I think he's a different sort of Golem, though. I'm not too sure, but I have him in custody."

I almost jumped or squealed, but was proud of myself for remaining professional. "He's a Mimic." I explained the difference we'd discovered in our research and how he could have gotten into Art's shop. "We found the real Art, too. The paramedics took him to the hospital, but he had a lot to say." I filled him in on the rest of what Art had told me.

"Meet me at the station. It seems we have some people we need to talk to."

Aramis

"Tell me why you didn't lead with the '*I used to be a big city detective*' line, son."

Sheriff Oliphant had come in nearly an hour ago with Blair on his heels.

I was back in the interrogation room—sans handcuffs—because they'd brought in a Mimic who had apparently confessed to accidentally killing who he thought was me—a Golem walking around with my face on. The deeper problem was obviously *why* he'd been planning to kill me and why there was a Golem walking around as me at all.

"I came here to get away from the detective life," I said simply because it was the truth. Had the itch to solve the murder put me in a chokehold? Yes. But I had not investigated...much.

"Well, that life followed you here," the sheriff said.

Wardwell was standing behind him, looking at me. The prettiest distraction I'd ever seen.

"And you have no idea why the deceased Golem would have been walking around looking like you?"

"Kenny has been sifting through the, uh, roster of enemies I'm aware of for a Golem. Other than that, I really don't."

Sheriff stood from his chair. "Well, the guy doesn't seem to know why he was sent here, or who actually did the sending. He's admitted to being sent to kill you and kidnapping Art, as well as killing your look alike because he thought it *was* you, and for framing you for the Golem murder."

"Hang on," Blair piped up from her spot in the corner. "If the Golem didn't know the Mimic, why did they both have sparrow tattoos? Wouldn't that signify they're from the same clan?"

"The clan could be huge for all we know." I shrugged. "Or, more likely, it's what connects them to whoever is against me."

"None of this is overly comforting," she grumbled.

"We'll figure it out, Wardwell."

She gave me a small smile. "Hey, what about Anon? Did the Mimic confess to the attack?"

"Now that's a peculiar one," Oliphant said, his bushy

brows furrowed. "I questioned him about that, but he insists he has no idea about any of it."

"You believe him?" Blair asked.

"I do. He confessed to killing someone and being hired to kill someone else. Another assault charge isn't going to make a difference."

"And is this the person who killed Steven as well?" Because I had a sudden sinking feeling it wasn't.

Sheriff Oliphant looked like he'd aged twelve years in the last week. "He claims that was not him, either."

"Someone coming to finish what the first two couldn't?" Blair guessed with a sour expression. "Frame you?" And I worried she was right.

"One thing at a time, darlin'." I knew the sheriff only said it to comfort her, but her shoulders did lose some of their tension, so I suppose it worked.

"Sheriff, am I free to walk Wardwell home?" I offered her a wry smile and she tried to return it. She needed rest, badly.

"You're free to go, son."

I reached for Blair's hand and her fingers were freezing. As I took off my overshirt and draped it across her shoulders, Oliphant cleared his throat.

"If I need any, ah, consulting," he said, "do you do that sort of thing?"

"I do!" Blair piped up, a genuine smile on her lips, traveling up to glitter in her eyes. Sheriff sighed, but he was almost grinning, too.

"Yeah, I'm learning I'd have to pay you *not* to consult," he complained, but we all knew he didn't mean it.

"I'll consider it," I said, sticking out my hand for him to shake.

"Please do."

Blair

The walk home was long and chilly, both of us exhausted but unwilling to part. Eventually, we made it to my front door and I could already tell Mom and my aunts were inside. I heard the Wardwell *Cackle of All Cackles* and knew Grandma was in there, too.

I tried to give Aramis his flannel shirt back, but he refused, and there was no way I was going to fight him on it. He bent and gave me a chaste kiss on the cheek.

"Can I bring you coffee tomorrow?"

I grinned from ear to ear. "Only if it's one of your new creations."

The smile he gave me made my knees weak. "Deal. Goodnight, Wardwell."

"Goodnight, Hawthorne."

Mom ambushed me the second I made it inside. Then everyone else joined in. They fussed over me, asked a thousand questions, and fed me the equivalent of three dinners before Mom kicked everyone out and sent my cousins up to bed. We talked over glasses of deep red wine before Mom went back to the inn and I climbed upstairs to draw a bath.

As I sank into the delectably warm water and let it soak all my tension away, my tired mind considered how much had changed in the last couple of weeks. It felt like nothing in Gloam Hollow would ever be the same again.

I sipped my wine and pressed my neck into the lip of the

tub, relishing a brief moment of peace before we needed to confront the next tragedy. Who had killed poor Steven, and why? Who was after Aramis? And how did it connect to Anon?

I soaked in the bath, sipping at my wine with Puck lying on the edge of the tub, his tail dragging through the bubbles. When the bubbles dissolved and the water grew tepid, I was teetering on the verge of a dreamlike state of consciousness. I climbed out of the bath and barely managed to put on a nightgown before I collapsed into bed.

As I drifted off to sleep, a thought occurred to me, playing on repeat in my dreams:

It is so often difficult to appreciate peace until it's disrupted.

TO BE CONTINUED

in

Gloam Hollow, Book Two:

MORTAL MAYHEM

Gloam HOLLOW

RECIPES

Blair's Autumn
Simmer Pot

add ingredients to a stovetop pot of boiling water,
cover, reduce heat to simmer all day
*lasts a few days

- 1 whole orange peel, sliced into strips.

- 2 tablespoons whole cloves

- 3 whole cinnamon sticks

- 1 tablespoon nutmeg

- 2 drops of vanilla extract

Aramis's
Smashing Pumpkin
Cocktail

Syrup:

- ½ cup sugar
- ½ cup water
- 1-3 cinnamon sticks

Cocktail:

- ¼ cup pumpkin puree
- 3 oz bourbon
- 2 oz pure maple syrup
- ¼ oz cinnamon syrup
- 1 oz orange liqueur
- 2 dashes orange bitters
- Orange peel twists (garnish)

Instructions

Syrup:

1. Place sugar, water, and cinnamon sticks in a small saucepan. Bring to a boil over medium heat, stirring occasionally.
2. Turn off the heat immediately. Let syrup sit until cooled to room temp.

*Mixture can be stored in a container for up to 3 weeks in the refrigerator.

Cocktail:

3. Fill a cocktail shaker halfway with ice.
4. Combine pumpkin puree, bourbon, maple syrup, cinnamon syrup, orange liqueur, and orange bitters in the shaker. Shake.
5. Fill two chilled cocktail glasses with fresh ice, and strain the cocktail into the two glasses.
6. Garnish with a twist of orange peel and a cinnamon stick

Mama Wardwell's Apple Crumble Muffins

Topping recipe

3 Tbsp. white sugar
3 Tbsp. brown sugar
1/2 cup + 2 Tbsp. of flour
1 tsp. cinnamon
1/4 tsp. of salt
6 Tbsp. of butter

Glaze

1 cup powdered sugar
3 Tbsp. milk

Muffin Recipe

2 3/4 cups of flour
2 cups of apples, chopped
into small cubes
1 cup of sugar
1 cup of milk
1 stick of butter, softened or
melted but not hot
1/3 cup of sour cream
2 large eggs
1.5 tsp. baking powder
1 tsp. salt
2.5 tsp. cinnamon
2.5 tsp. of vanilla

INSTRUCTIONS

- Preheat your oven to 425
- Mix together crumble topping ingredients in a bowl and fluff with a fork. Set aside.
- In a separate bowl, mix together dry muffin ingredients. Whisk to combine well.
- In a large bowl, mix together the wet muffin ingredients. *Ensure butter isn't hot, but soft.
- Slowly mix in dry muffin ingredients into the wet ingredients.
- Fold in chopped apples.
- Line muffin tins and then fill them 3/4 full
- Sprinkle on the crumble
- Bake for 18-20 minutes.
- As the muffins bake, combine glaze ingredients in a bowl. Set aside.
- Let muffins cool, then drizzle on the glaze

STONEWOOD
Coffee Shop On The Square

LACUNA'S
MAPLE CINNAMON LATTE

Ingredients:

- 1/4 cup hot espresso or strongly brewed coffee
- 1-2 tablespoons maple syrup
- 1/4 teaspoon vanilla extract
- Pinch ground cinnamon plus more for garnish
- 3/4 cup steamed milk (any kind)
- Maple sugar leaf from Toil & Truffle (decoration)

Instructions

1. Pour maple syrup, vanilla extract, and cinnamon into the bottom of a mug.
2. Pour in the hot espresso and stir to combine.
3. While holding the mug at a 45 degree angle, slowly pour the steamed milk in the center to fill the mug and add a thin layer of the foam to the top.
4. Decorate the top with an additional pinch of cinnamon and a maple sugar leaf

Blair  Wardwell's

FASHION BOARD

*The only thing she enjoys
about the magical Interweb

J.L. VAMPA

Jane Lenore (J.L.) Vampa is an author of Fantasy and Victorian Gothic fiction. She lives in the south with her musician husband and their littles who are just as peculiar as they are.

Be sure to follow JL on TikTok - @JLVampa